1

For the dozenth time in an hour, Nathan Stone stopped to catch his breath and wipe the sweat from his forehead. The heat, which the weather people had failed to predict until yesterday, four days after the start of his holiday, was mostly to blame for how he felt, but Nathan couldn't deny that being out of shape played a part as well.

He felt glad that he had chosen such a quiet location for his holiday as he sat on a moss-covered boulder a short distance from the bank of the river. There was no-one around to see him as he sweated and breathed heavily, and no-one to notice that it was almost five minutes before he felt sufficiently recovered to push himself up and continue his walk.

Fortunately, he had only a little farther to go before he reached his destination, the waterfall that cascaded down from the moor above the wooded valley through which he was trekking. Once he made it to the waterfall and got a picture to prove he had managed the four-mile walk, he could turn around and head back to the small hotel where he was staying.

The fact that it was likely to be another hour and a half, if not more, before he reached the hotel didn't bother him, nor that it would be dusk by then. He was on holiday and had all the time in the world — that wasn't quite true, he had nine days before he had to return to work, but that was as good as having all the time in the world — and he was having a good time, the first good time he could remember in a while.

He was surrounded by the beautiful countryside of Devon, he had no investigations to worry about — when not on holiday he was a detective inspector in the town of Branton, which meant he was surrounded by death and violence more often than he liked — and he had seen numerous animals and birds, including a few birds of prey. He had even seen a couple of foxes, or it might have been the same fox seen twice.

Foxes were not a surprising sight to him. Though he came from an urban environment, he had seen many a fox while working night shifts, there had even been one that made regular appearances in his back garden, when he had a back garden. He had lost the garden, along with the house it was attached to, in the arson attack that had killed his family.

It took him barely a second to get from foxes to his family, and a similar length of time to go from a reasonable mood to being overcome by grief. It had been less than a year since his wife and children perished in the flames that left him without a home or a family and his sense of loss remained as strong as ever, with only the occasional distraction to take his mind from it.

Fortunately, a distraction appeared just then to help him out. Out the corner of his eye, Nathan saw a blur of movement and automatically turned his head to try and identify it. His first thought was that it was a domestic cat, which would have been surprising enough given that they were several miles from the nearest house, but when the creature slowed, enabling him to see it better, he realised it was too big and the wrong colouring.

Many reports of 'beasts' roaming the moors had appeared online and in the news over the years, but they were always big cats, jaguars or similar-sized creatures. What he saw was bigger than a domestic cat, but far too small to have given rise to the stories he had heard. Nonetheless the size and colouring made it clear that he was looking at a wildcat of some kind.

The sight was so startling that for almost a minute all he could do was stare at the creature that, after its initial burst of speed, was now strolling casually along the riverbank.

Once he recovered from his surprise, Nathan fumbled to get his camera out of its case, so he could record the sighting. The noise of the camera turning on cut through the silence of the woods, though, and by the time Nathan got the camera up all he was able to snap was a blur as the feline darted away in alarm.

When he checked the picture, he saw that it was as bad as he had feared. If he showed it to anyone and tried to convince them that it was a wildcat, he would be looked at like he was trying to pass off a bright light in the sky as a UFO.

Disappointed, he remained where he was for a couple of minutes in case the cat was going to reappear. When it didn't, he continued to the waterfall, so he could get the picture he had been after in the first place. He then turned around to head back to his hotel, where he planned on getting some much-needed rest.

NATHAN BLINKED RAPIDLY to adjust his eyes to the sudden gloom and gave an involuntary shiver as he stepped from the blazing heat of outside into the foyer of The Moor's Edge hotel, where it was at least ten degrees cooler.

Cooler it might be, but it was also stuffier, and Nathan was glad to step into the path of a fan that was circulating air when he reached the reception counter. He couldn't help reflecting that if there had been a breeze while he was in the woods the day would have been almost perfect.

"Good evening, sir."

"Hi," Nathan returned the receptionist's greeting. "Could I get my key please, room thirty-four."

"Of course." The young man reached behind him to take down the key from the appropriate hook — The Moor's Edge still used metal keys, rather than the electronic keycards that more and more hotels were adopting. "You have a message, sir," he said, handing over a folded-up slip of paper along with the key.

"Thanks." Nathan took both the message and the key and left the foyer.

He waited until he reached his room on the third floor to read the message that had been left for him, not that he expected it to be anything private. It turned out to be nothing important. All it said was that his friend, Louisa Orchard, had been trying to get hold of him and was worried because she had only been able to get his answerphone.

A quick check of his phone revealed that he had two bars and an almost full battery, so he didn't know why Louisa hadn't been able to get hold of him. He reasoned that his signal must have disappeared while he was hiking through the countryside; given how far he had been from the village, where he only got half a signal, that seemed likely.

He debated whether to call his friend back but decided against it. He was sure she had only been calling to check up on him, so there was no reason for him to rush to get in touch. He would call her in a while, and there was every chance that she would try again to hold of him if she didn't hear from him quickly enough for her liking.

It had been the same every day since he arrived in Donningford, Devon, either Louisa or his sister had called to make sure he was okay. They, along with his friend and occasional partner, Detective Sergeant Stephen Burke, had cajoled and almost bullied him into taking this holiday, so he could get some rest and relaxation and start to put the loss of his family behind him, yet they couldn't help checking up on him constantly.

He knew why they felt the need to hear his voice at least once a day — they were afraid that he would reach a low point and harm himself. He was past the point of doing that, though. He couldn't say that he was okay with the murder of his family, he doubted he would ever be able to say that, but he no longer felt the intense grief over the death of his wife and kids that he had immediately following their loss, and he no longer wished to end his life and join them in whatever place a person went to after death.

He was too hot and sticky to deal with his friend and her concerns just then. He was more interested in cooling down after his walk. Stripping off, he headed into the small en-suite bathroom that had convinced him to take a double room rather than a single, so he could clean off the sweat from his hike in the sun and freshen up before he went down for dinner.

It wasn't his normal habit to take his phone with him when he went for a shower, but he thought it best to do so, just in case Louisa tried calling him again.

He wouldn't put it past her to call the local police and have them track him down if she went too long without being able to get hold of him.

2

"Hello, Mr Stone, what can I get you?"

Nathan scanned the array of drinks behind the barmaid, a move that was done more out of habit than out of interest since he already knew what he wanted. "I'll have a cider, please," he said finally.

"You can tell you've been out in the sun," Jennifer Pierson, the daughter of the couple who ran The Moor's Edge hotel remarked as she set the glass of cider in front of Nathan. "You've gone red. If you're not careful, you'll be peeling before you know it."

Nathan's smile held a touch of grimace for she was right, he had been burned by the sun. He had put cream on after his shower, but his skin was still tight and sore. "I got caught by surprise. I had sun cream on but didn't expect it to be as bad as it was. Plus, I ended up going further than I planned."

Now that he had stopped walking his muscles were beginning to stiffen up. He was sure he would barely be able to walk by morning, which only reminded him of how long it had been since he was last in decent shape. It wasn't that he was completely out of shape, but he couldn't remember when he had last walked for longer than half an hour at a stretch, and that done over flat terrain and usually at a casual pace. His hike to the waterfall and back had proved to be exercise he was unprepared for.

"Where did you go?" Jennifer, whom Nathan had got to know reasonably well over the past few days, asked.

"The waterfall from that picture in reception," Nathan told her. "I didn't intend going that far. I didn't realise how far it was to be honest. I just went for a walk in the woods and ended up following the path that runs alongside the river. Before I knew it, I'd been walking for over an hour and was at the waterfall. It was worth it, though, it's even more beautiful than the picture suggests, but I'm going to suffer for it tomorrow."

He might not have agreed with his sister or his friends when they all but bullied him into taking a holiday, but he couldn't deny that he felt better for it, even if he was stiff and sore. The first day of his holiday had been spent travelling down to Devon and settling into the hotel, and the second occupied with finding his way around the small community of Donningford. The past two days, though, when he considered his holiday to have really begun, he had felt himself relaxing as the weather improved and he began to put behind him, at least for a while, the loss of his family and the difficulties that had followed.

"You'd be surprised how often that happens," Jennifer remarked. "People intend only to go for a short walk and find that they've been out for hours and have done miles."

"It's so easy to lose track of time when surrounded by such beautiful scenery," Nathan said. "I've seen TV programs about the area, but they don't really show just how beautiful it is."

"Beautiful, yes, but it can also be dangerous to someone who doesn't know the area well. I hope you had the sense to stick to the paths."

"No worries there, the furthest I went from the path was about ten feet to get a better angle for a picture, and I made sure to keep the path in sight when I did."

"I'm glad to hear it. You wouldn't believe how many of our guests don't have enough sense to stick to the paths, even though we tell them to. So many of them have no appreciation of how easy it is to get lost, both in the woods and out on the moor, or how difficult it is to find the path again when they do get lost. It's worse on the moor. Even on a clear day like today you can get lost in a heartbeat. The moment you lose sight of the trail you're in trouble. There are few real landmarks out there and even an experienced hiker can get in trouble if they stray.

"Of course, being lost is only half the problem. People don't seem to realise how quickly they can be overcome by dehydration or heatstroke. Then there's the risk of them injuring themselves. A twisted ankle might not seem like a serious injury, but out on the moor it can cost you your life. Sorry, I'm not trying to scare you," Jennifer apologised. "But I've got a friend who volunteers with the local search and rescue, and he's got so many stories of people who've got themselves into trouble in the stupidest of ways, like trying to get close enough to a horse or deer to pet it.

"Would you like a refill?"

The sudden change in the conversation's direction surprised Nathan, though not as much as looking down and discovering that his glass was all but empty. "Please." He lifted the glass to his lips, so he could drain the remains of his cider, and then slid it across the bar to be refilled. He hadn't realised how thirsty he was.

"So," Jennifer took up the conversation again as she set the replenished drink in front of her sole customer, "did you see much of our local wildlife during your walk?"

"I did, as it happens," Nathan said. He forced himself to sip at his second cider, rather than gulping it like the first, as his still dry throat wanted him to. "I saw a few horses in the distance before I got into the woods, a deer, plenty of rabbits and a bunch of birds, even a couple of foxes. I might even have seen a wildcat," he said after a pause. "Do you get them in this area? Other than the supposed big cat sightings, I mean."

Jennifer didn't answer straightaway, instead she looked thoughtfully at Nathan as though trying to decide how best to respond to the question. "What did it look like?" she asked finally.

Nathan was quiet for a moment as he thought back to what he had seen. "It was bigger than a domestic cat, getting on for a metre-long including the tail, tawny coloured with black markings. It looked like a little leopard. I tried to take a picture of it, but it took off like it knew what I was doing and didn't want to be photographed. All I managed to get was a yellow blur that no-one's going to believe is a wildcat."

"That sounds like a wildcat," Jennifer agreed. "Don't ask me what species it is, though, or how common they are, I don't have a clue."

"No problem," Nathan said unconcernedly. "I was just after reassurance that I hadn't imagined it out of heat exhaustion or something."

"Well, I can't say for sure that isn't the case," Jennifer said teasingly. "But you're not the only person to say they've seen wildcats in the area, and everyone who says they've seen one has described it the same as you. One or two of them even have pictures that can almost be recognised as being of felines. If you're interested in them, you need to speak to my friend, I'll point him in your direction when he comes in later. When he's not volunteering with search and rescue, he's studying zoology and training to be a vet, so he knows as much about the local wildlife as anyone.

"If anyone can tell you about the cats, it's Floyd."

Nathan was tempted to tell her not to bother, not to put herself or her friend to any trouble. He couldn't deny that he was curious about the creature he had seen, however. If he could find out more about it, maybe even see it again, or, better yet, get a photograph that showed it for what it was, being 'encouraged' to take a holiday would have been worth it.

3

Nathan was halfway through the best cottage pie he had ever tasted when someone stopped at his table, casting a shadow over his meal. He looked up and found that the owner of the shadow was a young man of about twenty.

"Mr Stone?"

Nathan nodded. "That's right, I'm Nathan Stone," he said after swallowing the mouthful he was chewing on. "How can I help you?"

"Actually, I'm here to help you, Jenny said you're interested in the local wildlife. Floyd Mantle, mind if I join you?"

"Not at all, please do." Nathan gestured to the seat across from him. "Thanks for sparing the time."

Floyd grinned. "No problem, I'm always happy to talk about the local animals, it's my favourite subject. And as Jenny probably told you, I know as much as anyone about them. So, what is it you're interested in?"

"Wildcats," Nathan said after taking a sip of his cider. "I think I saw one this afternoon."

Floyd's grin broadened. "Did you manage to get a picture?"

Nathan shook his head. "Not a decent one anyway. The best I could manage was a blurry image of moving colour that could be just about anything."

"That's about all most people seem able to manage. The cats are too quick for them, especially when they're caught by surprise and not expecting to see something like that out there." Floyd reached into the pocket of his shirt and took out a photograph. "Is this the creature you saw?" he asked, setting the photograph down next to Nathan's plate.

Nathan chewed thoughtfully on a fresh mouthful of cottage pie while he examined the photo. "Yes," he said finally. "That looks like the cat I saw, what is it? And how did you manage to get such a clear picture of it?"

Floyd put down the pint of lager he had been sipping at and accepted the photo back. "It's an ocelot," he told Nathan. "I haven't been able to prove it yet, but I believe there's a trio of them living in the woods on the edge of the moor, two males and a female. I don't have a clue where they came from, they're not native to the UK, never have been — ocelots are from South America. Mind you, nothing makes sense about these cats. Ocelots usually aren't overly social, nor do they tackle large prey, but there have been several dead horses and deer found over the past six months that have clearly been the work of wildcats.

"As for the picture, it took me several lengthy sessions of waiting patiently in the same spot to get. I don't mind telling you, I was ready to give up and forget all about it when this chap came strolling down to the stream I had staked out, casual as you like, for a drink. He was there for several minutes and then he disappeared back into the trees. I tried following but he was gone."

"You say you don't have a clue where these ocelots came from, what about theories?" Nathan felt compelled to ask. He was a curious person and couldn't accept that these non-native creatures had just magically appeared in Devon. "You must have some thoughts about how these cats ended up here."

Floyd shrugged. "Who can say. Personally, I think they're from an illegal private collection; either they escaped or were released because the owner can't maintain it any longer. It's not something that's talked about openly, but I know it wouldn't be the first time that someone who owns an illegal collection of animals just let them go, either because they couldn't afford to run it anymore or because they were close to being caught. Most such animals die pretty quickly because they're not equipped to survive in the wild, even when the wild is as benign as it is here in the UK, but some manage to survive alright for a while."

It saddened Nathan to think that people would traffic in such animals, just to cage them for their own pleasure, and would then release them without a concern for whether they could survive when they no longer wanted them.

"Is anything being done to help the cats?" he asked.

Floyd looked bemused. "Like what? Right now, there's no need to do anything to help them, they're managing to look after themselves okay. Sure, they've killed the occasional horse or deer, but it's all been wild animals they've killed, and mostly rabbits and squirrels and other small things. So long as they're not attacking people or owned animals, there's no reason to do anything other than leave them alone.

"A few people around here, those that believe the cats exist, which isn't everyone, have suggested that something should be done about them — they either want them hunted down and killed, or they want them caught and put in a zoo or something. Nobody takes such suggestions seriously, though, and I doubt they will so long as most people aren't even willing to admit that the cats are really out there."

"Is there anywhere in particular that gives the best chance of seeing the cats? Are you more likely to see them on the moor or in the woods around the river?" Nathan asked.

"Why do you want to know where you can find them?" Floyd wanted to know, suspicion and concern in his voice, which Nathan couldn't blame him for.

"I'd like to see the cat again," Nathan told him honestly.

Floyd relaxed a little after studying the man across the table from him for a short while. "I hope you appreciate that these are dangerous animals. Under normal circumstances they're more likely to run away than attack, but if they're cornered or they feel threatened, or they're disturbed while feeding or mating, they will do some serious, perhaps even fatal, damage.

"Ocelots might not be as big as tigers or lions, but they can still be dangerous, especially if there's more than one."

"Don't worry, I have no intention of disturbing them. I just want to see the cat again, all three if I could, and maybe get a picture that actually shows what I'm looking at, so when I tell my friends I saw an ocelot, I'll have proof. Not only that but one of my friends runs a news and information website, I think she'd be interested in these ocelots, especially if she had an account from someone who saw them first-hand. Better yet, an account from someone like you, who knows about them. Would you be interested in speaking to her?" The website Louisa ran focused mostly on news and crime stories, but she was always looking for interesting or unusual stories to post, anything that might draw attention to her site.

"Sure. I'd be happy to speak to your friend about the ocelots," Floyd said with unbridled enthusiasm. "Obviously, I can't tell her anything about where the cats come from, but I'll tell her what I do know, both about ocelots in general and about the ones we have here in particular."

"That's okay, knowing Louisa, she'll make up a story about where they come from that will be better than whatever the truth is, either that or she'll leave it as a mystery. The readers of her site love a mystery, and the appearance of three ocelots on Dartmoor is definitely one. She'll get people interested enough to read whatever you do know about them, especially if you're able to provide good quality pictures to go with the story." Nathan knew people would be interested in the story because he was.

Why the story of three ocelots should interest him so much, he couldn't have said. He liked nature and animals as much as the next person, but it wasn't like him to go out of his way to interact with it.

The only answer he could come up with was his love of mysteries and the unknown, the love that had led to him joining the police force and then becoming a detective. In the absence of any other mystery to puzzle out the solution to, how three wildcats came to be on Dartmoor was all he had.

His wife had always said that he was happiest when his brain was occupied by an enigma.

"I've got four good, clear photographs, including this one." Floyd tapped the pocket that again held the picture he had shown to Nathan. "And about half a dozen others where you can make out the subject is an animal, but not what sort of animal it is. Have you got anything planned for the rest of the evening?"

The question caught Nathan by surprise. "I've got a phone call to make, but other than that my evening's free, why?"

"If you're really interested in seeing the cats, I can take you to where you're most likely to see them."

4

Exhilarated, Nathan strolled along the narrow path that meandered through the woods as he headed slowly back to the hotel. For just short of two hours he had lain motionless in the undergrowth, Floyd Mantle at his side, until finally not one but two of the ocelots had shown up, stalking silently down to the stream to slake their thirst.

Less than twenty feet had separated him from the wildcats — the female and one of the males, according to Floyd, not that Nathan could tell them apart, even with Floyd pointing out the differences between them in a whisper. He had been close enough to get more than a minute of video as well as several good quality photographs.

If someone had told him before he arrived in Donningford that he would get that close to a pair of wildcats, he never would have believed them.

"...go on much longer."

Nathan stopped the moment he heard the voice — male, angry and fearful. He didn't want to intrude on a private conversation, nor did he want to stay in a place where he could, however unwillingly, overhear one. Unfortunately, he had few options, and none of them were good: he couldn't stay where he was, because that would leave him able to hear the conversation, and he couldn't turn and head back the way he had come, because that would put him farther from the hotel, without knowing of an alternative route he could take to get there.

The only option that seemed practical was for him to continue to the hotel and ignore the conversation as best he could. He hoped that once whoever was out there realised they were not alone they would stop talking until he was gone.

"If you don't leave him soon, he's going to kill you."

"It's not as bad as that." A female voice that time, one that tried and failed to sound confident. *"He was sorry the moment he hit me. It's my fault for making him angry. I should know better by now. Anyway, he said it won't happen again."*

"How many times has he said that?" the male voice asked, its owner fighting, and only just succeeding, to remain calm. *"It's always the same. He gets angry over something stupid, lashes out at you, apologises and swears it'll never happen again, and then he manages to make you feel responsible for it all. He's put you in hospital twice, Tracey, and broken God knows how many bones over the years; then there's all the bruises and other injuries. Honestly, it's a miracle he hasn't done you permanent harm. It's only a matter of time 'til he does, and you know I couldn't stand it if anything happened to you.*

"What's that?" the man said suddenly.

Nathan was doing his best not to listen to the conversation taking place around the bend in the path, but it simply wasn't possible to block the voices out completely, especially with his innate curiosity about everything that happened around him. What made it harder to block out and ignore was the familiarity of the conversation; the situation being described was one he had heard far too often — it was a tale of domestic abuse and he knew all the possible outcomes.

"Do you think there could be someone out here?"

Nathan heard the alarm in the man's voice mirrored in the woman's and hastened his pace. It didn't surprise him that she was concerned about the possibility of there being someone else out there. Based on the small amount he had heard, she was probably terrified that her husband or partner was out there, spying on her. The sooner he caught up to them, the sooner he could allay the woman's worries.

"It's probably just an animal, a badger or a fox," the man responded, his initial concern fading rapidly as common-sense took over.

"You'd better go," the woman told him, urgency in her voice. *"It might be..."*

The man cut her off. *"What would he be doing out here? He never comes out here, that's why you picked the spot, because he isn't likely to find us."*

"Still," she said uncertainly. *"You'd better go, just in case. If it is David, and he finds us together..."* Her voice tailed off and the silence that followed held more meaning than anything she might have said.

Nathan rounded the bend in the path in time to see the back of the conversation's male participant disappear into the gloom up ahead. The man was too far away to be recognised, assuming he was someone he had encountered during his holiday, but Nathan had no such difficulty when it came to the conversation's female participant, she stood in the middle of the path as though she wanted to be seen.

Since he was practically on top of her the moment he came around the bend, Nathan easily recognised the woman as Tracey Pierson, the wife of the owner of The Moor's Edge hotel. The beginning of a bruise was visible under her right eye and across her cheek and Nathan was sure that come morning she was going to need plenty of makeup to conceal it.

"Sorry, I didn't mean to startle you," he apologised when she jumped at his sudden appearance. Her surprise was mixed with relief, which he could understand if she had been afraid that he was her husband, and she was about to be caught in the middle of a secret conversation with someone she wasn't supposed to be seeing.

"That's okay, Mr Stone," Tracey Pierson said with forced calm and a smile that was a bit too shaky to be as pleasant and welcoming as it was meant to be. "You caught me by surprise, that's all. I didn't expect to come across anyone out here, especially not a guest. I was getting some air; I like to wind down after a busy day with a stroll."

The story might have been more convincing, Nathan thought, if she hadn't been looking around nervously as she delivered it. When her eyes did stop, they fixed tellingly on where the path disappeared into the gloom on its way back to the village, on the spot where Nathan had last seen the retreating back of the man Tracey Pierson had brought to such an out of the way place to hold a conversation with.

"You certainly picked a nice spot to get some air," Nathan said casually, looking around admiringly at the scenery. "I was doing something similar myself. Jennifer's friend, Floyd, showed me a spot, it's a bit of a walk from here, where I was able to get closer than I would have believed possible to a pair of the wildcats that seem to have made a home for themselves around here."

A wan smile touched Tracey Pierson's lips. "I imagine he was thrilled," she said. "As excited as he gets about those creatures, you'd think they were his pets. There are times when I think he likes them more than he likes Jenny, and the two of them have been friends since they were little kids."

"Are you heading back to the hotel?" Nathan asked after a moment, when it became clear that there was nothing else for the two of them to talk about. "I'd be happy to walk with you if you want some company."

Tracey shook her head. "No, my..." She quickly stopped herself before she could finish what she was about to say and started again. "No, thank you, I like the peace and quiet at this time of the night. Besides, if you don't get back soon, you're likely to find yourself locked out, assuming David hasn't locked the door already, which he probably has. He usually locks up around midnight and goes to bed."

"As pleasant as it is out here, I wouldn't want to spend the night in the open air," Nathan said. "At least not without an opportunity to plan for it. Enjoy your walk." With that he hurried away as quickly as his legs would carry him and his eyes could make out the path.

It hadn't occurred to him that by staying out so late he might find himself in the position of being locked out of the hotel. He was sure he would be able to get someone to open up and let him in, nonetheless he hoped the doors were still open, so he didn't have to disturb anyone.

5

Tired though he was after his late night of nature watching, Nathan woke on the dot of five-thirty. He had been waking at that time for so long that he did so regardless of whether he had an alarm set, or even if he had a reason for getting up.

He was halfway out of bed before he remembered that there was no reason for him to get up. Even so, he had to force himself to slip back under the covers and close his eyes; he didn't hold out much hope of being able to get back to sleep, but he couldn't see the point in getting up if he didn't need to, dozing was a better idea.

Despite his doubts, sleep did steal over him again for a couple more hours, until he was wrenched awake by a scream that filled the hotel from the cellar to the rafters.

Nathan was out of bed and at the door of his room before he fully registered what it was that had woken him. Fortunately, his brain kicked into gear as he was turning the knob to open the door; he slept in his boxer shorts and, regardless of the cause of the scream that had woken him, he didn't think it a good idea for him to leave the room dressed — undressed — as he was.

Turning away from the door he grabbed up the first pair of trousers he came to and pulled them on, followed by a t-shirt. He didn't waste any more time after that and left the room with nothing on his feet to hurry along the passage to the stairs, which he descended two and three at a time.

When he reached the ground floor he followed the sounds of distress to the rear of the hotel, past the dining room and into the kitchen. He had to stop almost immediately before he bumped into the uniformed constable who stood just inside the kitchen, talking to a trio of clearly distressed people.

Nathan had enough experience, both from his years as a detective and from his own traumas, to guess at what had caused the scream that had woken him. He was sure that the constable had just delivered the worst news that a person could receive — someone was dead.

Two of the three people being spoken to by the constable were known to Nathan, they were Jennifer and David Pierson. The third member of the trio was a stranger to Nathan, though he guessed from the white chef's outfit he wore that the man was one of the hotel's cooks.

"Is everything alright?" Nathan asked.

Clearly surprised, the constable spun around at the question. "Who are you?" he demanded.

"Nathan Stone, I'm a guest," he said. "I was woken by a scream, is everything alright?"

"There's been an incident, Mr Stone," the constable said in a serious voice, containing his suspicion and his surprise with an effort. "I have everything under control, but if you wouldn't mind taking a seat in the dining room, I'll need to speak to you and the other guests shortly."

"Of course, no problem, happy to help," Nathan said agreeably. As a police officer himself, he wasn't about to hinder the constable's work without a good reason.

He left the kitchen, but before following the constable's instructions and heading to the dining room he made his way back upstairs, so he could finish getting dressed. When he did make it to the dining room he took a seat at the bar, a position that would allow him to see all his fellow guests once they joined him, without it being obvious that he was observing them.

NATHAN HAD BEEN IN the restaurant, which had slowly filled up with the hotel's guests and staff, for a little over three quarters of an hour, time enough for him to make some toast and to be on his second cup of coffee, when the constable entered the room.

"Ladies and gentlemen. Ladies and gentlemen." The constable raised his voice to be heard over the conversations taking place between the guests, all of whom were curious about the reason for their summons to the restaurant. "First of all, I'd like to thank you all for your patience, and apologise for the necessity of having you all interrupt your holidays in our usually peaceful little village. Now, I don't want to upset or distress any of you but Tracey Pierson, the wife of the owner of this hotel, has been found dead." The news produced a chorus of shocked cries. "I'm sure many of you are wondering why I have gathered you here, since most of you barely knew Mrs Pierson."

From what Nathan could see, it wasn't just the guests who were wondering why they had been gathered together, the staff were wondering the same thing.

"The cause of Mrs Pierson's death is currently unknown," the constable continued. "That, combined with the fact that her body was found in a place where she wouldn't normally have been, means it is necessary that I speak to you all to determine your movements last night, as well as anything you might know about the last movements of Mrs Pierson."

"Are you trying to tell us she was murdered?" A voice boomed from the far corner of the dining room, where a beefy gentleman sat, glaring at the uniformed constable. "Surely you don't think any of us are involved, we barely knew the woman. You should be looking at the locals, they're far more likely to have a reason to kill her. My wife and I are here on holiday, you can hardly believe either of us killed her."

In a room of diverse people, it was almost to be expected that someone would react as that gentleman had. It was human instinct to want to deny a connection to a possible murder, and hardly indicative of guilt. Despite that, Nathan couldn't help shifting on his stool, so he could study the man and his wife better.

The man, whom Nathan had seen around the hotel during his stay, though he hadn't heard his name, was large, both in height and breadth. He was about half a foot taller than Nathan's five-eleven, and heavier by several stone; it might be mostly fat now, but Nathan was sure it had all been muscle once. He was equally sure that the man was no stranger to violence, he could see it in his eyes.

The next thing Nathan noticed was the ruddiness of the man's cheeks and the spider's web of broken veins across his face, which suggested he was accustomed to drinking often and heavily.

By contrast, the man's wife might as well not have been there. It was clear from even a quick glance that she was used to living in her husband's shadow, and any desire she may have once had to step out from it was long gone. Where her husband was tall and heavy-set, she was neither; even seated she was almost a head shorter, and so thin that she appeared starved.

It wasn't just her lack of stature that made it easy for her to be overlooked, her position at the table meant that her husband's bulk all but hid her from the other people in the dining room.

With an effort, Nathan forced his attention away from the table in the corner and back onto the constable, who was responding to what had been said.

"Until her body has been examined by the pathologist, we simply don't know how or why Mrs Pierson died," he said. "Since that's the case, we need to speak to each of you in turn to establish where you were during the night and what, if anything, you know about the situation.

"I appreciate that this is likely to take some time, and be an annoying interruption to your holidays, but I hope you will all be patient and bear with me."

6

Nathan ignored his stomach as it grumbled about the lack of a proper breakfast — three slices of toast had done little more than blunt his hunger — and concentrated on the email he was getting ready to send.

He was still in the dining room, as were the other guests and staff yet to be interviewed by Constable Havers, who had got around to introducing himself only after he had finished everything else he had to say.

It felt strange to be on the other side of a situation he was so familiar with. Having some knowledge of what was going on, though, made him more tolerant than the others in the room, many of whom were shifting uncomfortably in their seats or making unhappy comments in low undertones.

He was not alone in occupying himself with his phone, nearly everyone in the room was, even those who were complaining to their neighbours about the wait. The others were almost certainly more competent than he, however; it had taken him five minutes to remember the instructions he had been given for emailing someone from his phone, and then almost half an hour to write the email as he pecked slowly at the screen — he was not a natural typist and had to hunt down every letter.

When he was finally finished, Nathan hit the send button, dispatching the email to his friend, Louisa. He had no sooner done that than the door to the dining room swung open to admit Constable Havers. Nathan immediately turned his attention to the constable in case he was to be the next one called.

"Elizabeth Creek?" Constable Havers stared around the dining room, which by now had lost half its occupants. "I'm looking for a Ms Elizabeth Creek," he said, scrutinising each of the women in turn, as though he could tell which of them was the one he was after just by looking.

Nathan was a little disappointed that he wasn't going to be the next one to be questioned, he would have liked the opportunity to get on with his holiday, not that he currently had any plans for how he was going to spend his day. Fortunately, there was plenty of coffee available and he had his phone; he might not be the most proficient with it, but he could at least keep himself occupied with the reading app his sister had installed for him.

"That's me, I'm Elizabeth Creek," a timid, almost scared voice said as a woman of middle years, with thin brown hair, greying at the roots, and over-sized spectacles got hesitantly to her feet.

Automatically, Nathan ran his eyes over the woman, as he had each person taken away for questioning. No matter how hard he tried, he couldn't entirely turn off his professional instincts.

He suspected that he was doing Elizabeth Creek a disservice, but his first impression was that she perfectly fit the image of a stereotypical librarian, one who was prim and proper, and for whom silence truly was golden. Fear was the dominant emotion on the woman's face, which didn't surprise Nathan, he was sure this was her first experience with the police; he doubted that she had even been a victim of a crime, let alone a suspect in one. There was a hint of excitement there as well, though, and he suspected that she couldn't wait to get home and tell her small circle of friends all about being questioned over a suspicious death. It was almost certainly the most interesting thing that had happened to her.

It only took Nathan a few moments to complete his observations of Elizabeth Creek, but that was time enough for the lady to reach the door and follow Constable Havers out of the dining room. No sooner had the door swung closed behind them than his phone rang; the vibrations made it dance along the bar and he had to grab for it to keep it from falling to the floor.

A glance at the screen revealed that it was Louisa calling him, which he assumed meant she had read his email. It was too much of a coincidence for her to be calling him just then if she hadn't.

"Hi, Lou," Nathan answered the phone in a low voice. Unlike others in the dining room who had conducted telephone conversations with no regard for who might be able to overhear them, he preferred not to disturb his fellow detainees.

"Is that footage you sent me real?" Louisa asked without preamble. She knew Nathan was generally a serious person, but she couldn't help wondering if he had developed a sense of humour and was playing a prank of some kind on her.

"It's real," Nathan assured her. "And it's less than twenty-four hours old. I took it and the photographs myself just last night."

There was silence for several long moments and then Louisa said, "You're telling me you have proof that there's a pair of wildcats, ocelots according to your email, living on Dartmoor? How's that possible?"

"No idea," Nathan told her. "Apparently no-one knows where they came from, they just appeared about six months ago. And it's not a pair of ocelots, it's a trio, according to the young man who helped me get the footage I sent you; he reckons they're siblings."

"This just gets better and better," Louisa said. "I take it you're okay with me using your name in the story. What about the young man..." there was a brief pause as she consulted the email she had received, "Floyd Mantle? Do you think he'll be okay with being named in the story?"

"Yes. I did mention that you might be interested in doing a story about him and the ocelots, and he was fine with it; actually, I think he quite liked the idea."

"How about helping me get more footage of the cats and trying to figure out where they came from, and how they came to be on the moor? Do you think he'll be okay with that?"

"You're thinking of coming down here?" Nathan asked. He had been thinking more of a telephone interview between Louisa and Floyd, or perhaps an exchange of emails, he hadn't expected her to think about leaving Branton, not for the sake of a single story that was more a matter of casual interest than major news.

"Of course, how else am I going to write the story properly, use you as a freelance reporter?" Louisa asked, amused. "You're a good detective, but I've seen your reports, they're as dry as a desert. You'd bore my readers in less than a paragraph. Besides, you're biased. I'm better off with you as a witness."

Nathan could hardly fault her thinking, he did make a better witness than a reporter since his position as a detective inspector would lend credence to his account, but he took issue with her comment about his reports. His reports were dry because they only contained facts, not because he couldn't write with style; his superiors didn't appreciate creative writing on official reports.

"After all the stories over the years about lone big cats living around the country, this is the first time anyone's been able to produce solid imagery. It's like getting a clear picture of a UFO." It was all Louisa could do to contain her excitement. "Have they got any rooms available at the hotel you're at?"

"Sure, they're not full." Nathan wasn't sure how he felt about his friend coming down to join him on his holiday. She might say she was coming down to work on the story of the ocelots, but he was sure that at least part of her reason for coming to Devon was to keep an eye on him. She hadn't said as much when he called her the previous evening, but he knew she had been unhappy about not hearing from him for hours after she tried to get hold of him. "It might not be the best time for you to come down, though."

"Why's that?"

Nathan was reluctant to tell Louisa what was going on, knowing that it would only give her an extra reason to come to Donningford. He didn't think it a good idea to have her come down without knowing what was going on, however, so he quickly filled her in on the little he knew.

"Sounds like you've found some excitement to stop you getting bored down there," Louisa remarked.

"I was happy enough with just the scenery to enjoy," Nathan said. "I could do without this."

"I'm sure you could. Is there anything you'd like me to bring down for you?"

"No, thanks, I've got everything I need."

"In that case I'll see you in a few hours." Before she had even ended the call, Louisa was thinking about what she would need to take with her, and what she would need to do before she could leave for Devon.

7

Certain that he was the most relaxed and unconcerned of those faced with the prospect of being questioned about a suspicious death, Nathan followed Constable Havers from the dining room. All those who had preceded him had displayed some form of stress or anxiety, whether it be a nervous tremor, a stammer when they spoke, or overcompensation in the form of belligerence and bluster, and the three who remained were no better.

"If you wouldn't mind stepping in here, Mr Stone," Constable Havers said, pushing open a door and stepping aside.

Nathan realised the moment he stepped through the door that they were in the manager's office. It was small, smaller than some cells he had seen, with most of the space taken up by a distressed-looking desk and a pair of worn, leather swivel chairs.

While Nathan took the seat closest to him, Havers moved around the desk to take the other.

"I apologise for the delay in talking to you, Mr Stone," Constable Havers said. "I hope you understand that this is a situation I am not experienced in dealing with, and there's a lot for me to do, most important of which is questioning all the guests. Not that I think any of you had anything to do with Mrs Pierson's death," he said hurriedly, as though afraid he might have given offence. "I don't even know yet that there is a reason for thinking that anyone had anything to do with the death."

Nathan was tempted to help the constable out, since he was not only inexperienced, as he had admitted, but also obviously unsure what he should do or say. He suspected the older man would not appreciate unsolicited help, however, so he kept quiet.

"I've asked you in here, Mr Stone," Constable Havers said finally, "because early this morning, the body of Tracey Pierson was found. The cause of her death is not considered suspicious at present, I hope to have confirmation of that soon, but her body was found in a place where she shouldn't have been. I should say a place she wasn't expected to be. I assume you know that Tracey Pierson is the wife of David Pierson, the owner of this hotel."

"I do, she was on the reception when I checked in the other day and introduced herself."

"Okay." Havers made a note of that on a pad that sat in front of him. "Did you know the Piersons before coming here on holiday?"

"Not at all. I didn't even speak to anyone at the hotel ahead of my arrival. I found the hotel online and booked through the website."

Another note was made. "Can you tell me when you last saw Mrs Pierson, and where?"

"I saw her last night," Nathan said without hesitation. Even if the encounter hadn't been recent enough to still be fresh in his mind, he had had plenty of time to think about the questions that were likely to be asked of him while he waited in the dining room. "It was somewhere between midnight and one a.m., I'm not sure of the exact time. I saw her in the woods about a mile from the hotel. I was on my way back here when I encountered her. She said she was out for some fresh air.

"I did ask if she wanted me to walk back to the hotel with her, but she said no, and advised me to get back quickly or I'd be locked out for the night."

"I see." There was no disguising the suspicion in Havers' voice as he leant forward slightly. "What were you doing out in the woods at that time of the night?" he asked. "It seems a little late to be walking around the countryside."

"Normally, I'd agree with you." Nathan ignored the constable's suspicion. Given how inexperienced he was, Nathan was sure he suspected everyone he had spoken to and would continue to do so until he either had a definite suspect or a good reason to discount someone as a suspect. "I had a reason for being out there, though. I was interested in finding out more about the ocelots you have living around here and was told of a spot where I might be able to see them."

"Ocelots?" Havers looked puzzled for a moment, but then his expression cleared. "Oh, you mean the wildcats that are supposed to be up on the moor."

"There's no supposed about it," Nathan said. "I saw them with my own eyes, I even got photos and video of them, so I can show my friends."

"Many people claim to have seen those cats," Havers remarked, unconvinced. "Many of them also claim to have photographs of them. None of that really matters right now, however. What does is whether you have anyone who can confirm your reason for being out in the woods after midnight, and the time you returned to the hotel, which was?"

"It was a little after one when I got back to the hotel, ten past by my watch by the time I got anyone to open the door to let me in. As for someone who can vouch for me, I was with a local by the name of Floyd Mantle, he's the one who took me out to see the cats. I imagine you know him." It was an assumption on Nathan's part that because of the small size of the community the constable would know most, if not all, the people who lived there, but one that was soon proven accurate.

"I know Floyd," Havers said. "He can confirm your encounter with Mrs Pierson and the time you returned to the hotel, can he?"

"Unfortunately not," Nathan said, sure that that was going to be a problem. He knew he could be wrong but based on the small amount he had been told, he suspected the body of Tracey Pierson had been found in the woods. "Mr Mantle and I parted company a little after midnight, when the ocelots left the stream where we were watching them; Floyd wanted to try and follow the cats to see if he could find out where they have their lair, while I was more than ready to come back to the hotel, having got the photos I was after.

"He can confirm when we parted company, however, and Jennifer Pierson can confirm the time I arrived back here, she was the one who let me in."

"Even if they can confirm those times, Mr Stone, that still leaves you with roughly an hour unaccounted for, and right now you appear to have been the last person to have seen Mrs Pierson, alive at least."

"Not unaccounted for, constable," Nathan said. He had no reason to worry, since he knew he had had nothing to do with the death of Tracey Pierson, nonetheless, he couldn't help feeling a slight concern that he was the last person to see her alive. If it should turn out that the death was suspicious, he would immediately become the prime suspect. Fortunately, he was sure that if the death was suspicious the case would be put in the hands of someone both more senior and more experienced, and he would then quickly be removed from the list of suspects. "It took me all of that time to get back to the hotel from the spot Floyd took me to."

Constable Havers was silent for several long moments as he thought about what he had been told, and what his next step should be. Finally, he said, "Did you see anyone else in the woods last night?"

"Not precisely."

"What's that supposed to mean?"

"It means I saw the back of someone, a man," Nathan said.

"Could you identify him?"

Nathan shook his head. "Sorry, no. I literally only saw his back. It was enough to tell that he was male, but that's it. I didn't even get a look at his hair. I came around a bend in the path as he was disappearing into the gloom up ahead, I barely got a glimpse of him."

"Where was he, and what was he doing? And what time was this?"

"I could take you to where it was, but I'm not sure I could describe it. As for what he was doing, when I saw him he was leaving Mrs Pierson. She was standing in the path when I came around the bend, and he was walking away from her."

"Why would Mrs Pierson be meeting someone in the woods after midnight?" Havers asked, though it was clear that he was asking the question of himself rather than of Nathan.

Despite the question not being directed at him, Nathan answered it. "I believe they met in the woods at that time because they were having an affair."

Havers stared at the man across from him for almost a full minute before he said anything. "You've been here just a few days, and you encountered Mrs Pierson in the woods only briefly, according to you, so what makes you think she was having an affair with the man you glimpsed? I've known Tracey for a number of years, and at no time has there been even a suggestion that she has been anything but faithful to David."

That didn't mean anything in Nathan's opinion; people who had affairs had to be both clever and careful, especially when the person being cheated on was prone to violent behaviour, as was the case based on what he had overheard. Those who weren't got caught quickly, with potentially serious consequences.

He would have been willing to bet that no matter how well Havers thought he knew the Piersons, he was as much in the dark about David Pierson's violent behaviour as he was about Tracey Pierson's affair.

"I overheard them," Nathan said simply, before going on to recount what he had overheard last night.

"Great, so now it seems as though this might not be an accidental or natural death," Havers said unhappily in a low voice, speaking to himself. "And I've already got two possible suspects."

NATHAN FOUND HIMSELF conflicted when he finally left the office. On the one hand, he was glad to have the interview over with — he suspected he would be interviewed again, by someone more competent, if it was determined that the death of Tracey Pierson was murder, but that was a worry for another time — so he could return to his holiday, while on the other he was unhappy to be on the scene of an unexplained death without being involved in the investigation.

He was too used to overseeing whatever investigations were happening around him, or at least being kept in the loop, to be happy about leaving one to someone else, especially when he doubted that he would know the investigating officers and couldn't be sure of their competency.

8

Louisa Orchard slowed as she approached The Moor's Edge hotel but a quick glance at the car park at the side of it revealed that it was full. Since that was the case she kept on going until she found a space up the street from the hotel.

"Two hours and eleven minutes," she said with satisfaction after a glance at the clock on the dashboard of her car. "And Google said it'd take almost three hours to get here." She smiled, knowing that the difference between the projected journey time and how long it had actually taken her to get there lay in the fact that she didn't always stick to the speed limit.

It only took her a minute to make her way back up the street to the hotel, where she discovered there was a genuine bell on the reception counter for summoning assistance, rather than a button attached to an electronic bell as was common in newer and more modern hotels. She suspected the quaintness stemmed from the hotel not having the money to modernise, rather than a deliberate attempt to provide an old-fashioned air, but that didn't stop her appreciating it.

"Good afternoon, can I help you?"

The voice of the young woman who appeared in response to the ringing of the bell was brittle, a clear indication, if Louisa had needed one, that something was up.

Nathan had told her only the bare minimum of what was going on, so she couldn't help wondering what the young woman's connection was to the body that had been found: was she merely an employee or was she related. Her curiosity was instinctive, stemming from the fact that she was a freelance journalist who spent her life looking into anything and everything that happened around her.

"Hello, yes, I've got a room booked, the name's Orchard," Louisa said. The look of consternation that crossed the face of the young woman didn't surprise her; under the circumstances, she was sure the last thing the hotel wanted was a new guest, who might either get in the way or complicate whatever investigation was taking place.

"I, uh, of course, let me just check," Jennifer Pierson said, forcing aside her surprise. She wasn't expecting anyone, the next booking she was aware of was for Friday, and it was only Wednesday.

It didn't take her long to find the booking. It had only been made a few hours before, which explained why she wasn't aware of it; checking for new bookings had understandably slipped her mind with everything that was going on, but that didn't explain why someone had made a last-minute booking for the middle of the week.

"Okay, I have you here, Ms Orchard," Jennifer said. "You're booked in for a single room for three nights and you've paid in advance, so if you'd like to sign the register, I'll give you your key." She produced the register from under the counter and then turned to find the right key from the hooks behind her. "Thank you." She took the register back once it had been signed and held out the key. "Your room is number twenty-three, on the second floor. Do you need any help with your luggage?"

"No thanks, I can manage," Louisa said, bending to pick up her bags, one of which held her untidily packed clothes, while the other, more carefully packed, contained her laptop and her camera, the vital equipment of her profession.

As she left the reception counter and made for the stairs, so she could ascend to her room, she wondered if her website was going to be okay while she was away. She had left it in the hands of the journalism and computer studies student she had hired to help her run the site, and while Kelly Hancock was a capable young woman, she had not been left in charge of the site before.

Dartmoor was not the back of beyond, so she should be able to keep an eye on the site and provide help if Kelly encountered any difficulties, but she worried about maintaining a mobile phone or wi-fi signal that would enable her to stay in touch with her assistant.

Jennifer Pierson watched the hotel's newest guest as she walked away from the counter. She was torn over whether she should call her back and tell her what had happened that morning. It was possible, she thought, that the woman would want to cancel her stay if she knew there had been a death that was under police investigation.

Two of the guests who had been questioned that morning had made it clear that as soon as they were permitted to leave, they would be going, and that they expected to receive refunds for their stays.

"Ms Orchard," she called out when the woman started up the stairs. She hurried around the counter and across the foyer. She was reluctant to broach the subject of what had happened to her mother, but she thought it best to tell Louisa Orchard what the situation at the hotel was; it was better for her to hear about it from a staff member than for her to get a garbled version from a guest or someone else.

"Yes?" Louisa turned back to the young woman.

Jennifer hesitated for a moment, unsure how to say what she had on her mind. "I think you should know, there's a police investigation underway at the hotel."

"What sort of investigation?" Louisa decided not to reveal that she already knew about the investigation.

"There was a death overnight. Not here in the hotel, and not one of our guests," Jennifer said hurriedly, hoping to reassure Louisa Orchard and keep her from making a snap decision. "The police are investigating to make certain of the cause of death. There shouldn't be any reason for you to be inconvenienced in any way, and the investigation shouldn't affect your holiday, but I thought you should know, before you start to wonder why there are police officers around the hotel."

Louisa accepted the information with a quick bob of her head and then made to continue up the stairs.

"If you'd prefer to cancel your booking," Jennifer went on, ignoring the fact that she was now speaking to the back of her guest. "We'll be happy to give you a full refund."

"That's not necessary," Louisa said over her shoulder. "I'll be sticking around. I may need the room I've booked for more than three nights, is that going to be a problem?"

It was a moment before Jennifer could answer. She was astonished that the lady before her not only didn't want to cancel her stay but might want to extend it. "No, of course not," she said when she recovered. "That won't be a problem at all, just let us know when you've decided if you're going to need the room for longer. And if you need anything during your stay, don't hesitate to ring through to reception, we'll do everything we can to help."

LOUISA REACHED THE second floor and room twenty-three in just a couple of minutes. She nudged the door open with a foot after unlocking it and stepped inside.

"Cosy," she commented to herself, looking around the room.

Cosy was certainly an apt description. The room was just about large enough for the single bed, wardrobe and bedside cabinet it held, with enough space for her to walk down the side of the bed to the window — if she had been much larger than she was, and she was pretty slim, it would have been difficult. There was no desk, and nowhere to sit other than the bed, but despite the lack of space and limited furniture, she did have to admit that the room was good for the money; the bed looked comfortable and the wardrobe and bedside cabinet were well-made, if obviously a couple of decades old.

Louisa wasn't bothered by the lack of a desk or anywhere proper to sit. So long as she had access to the internet, and Nathan had assured her that the hotel had an excellent wi-fi connection, she could manage. Much of her best work had been done at places other than a desk. Most had been done while dressed in an over-sized jumper, her favourite item of clothing, and relaxing either on the sofa or on her bed.

Opening the door of the wardrobe, Louisa casually tossed the rucksack inside and then set her other bag on the bed, so she could dig out the charger for her laptop. Once she had the laptop plugged in and connected to the hotel's wi-fi, so she could receive any emails that might need her attention, she went looking for her friend, sure that it wouldn't take her long to find him, not in such a small village.

9

If Nathan had known that his friend was there and looking for him, he might have returned to the hotel. He didn't expect her for several hours, though, so after his interview with Constable Havers he decided to take advantage of it being another hot and sunny day to go for a walk along the river, this time heading in the opposite direction to where he had gone yesterday.

Even if he had wanted to return to the woods in search of the ocelots, he couldn't have; the police had much of the woods in the immediate vicinity of the hotel cordoned off while the investigation into Tracey Pierson's death continued. He hadn't seen much evidence of an investigation beyond the tape warning people to stay away from the area, but he suspected that that was because Constable Havers appeared to be on his own and was waiting for support to arrive.

Instead of going into the words or out onto the moor, he followed the river to a small lake, where he spent the afternoon watching a variety of birds, most of which he couldn't identify, feeding and cooling themselves in the water.

He stayed there for a couple of hours, enjoying the view, and an ice-cream from a nearby van, before making his way back to the hotel so he could freshen up before dinner.

"HELLO, NATE," LOUISA greeted her friend as he joined her at the table where she was waiting for her dinner. "You've caught the sun in the last few days," she remarked, noting how much darker he had become since she last saw him, barely half a week ago.

"You don't realise how much sun you're getting just walking around, not until you take a proper look at yourself," Nathan said. He was several shades darker today than he had been yesterday, something he had only noticed when he stripped off to get in the shower. "How are you?" he asked. "How was the drive down?"

Louisa waited until Nathan had given his order to the waiter who appeared at his elbow to respond to his question. "I'm good, thanks. Of course, we only spoke this morning, so there hasn't been much chance for change. As for the drive down, it was alright, pleasant enough. Quite boring really, but at least the scenery during the last part was nice to look at. The only excitement I had, if you can call it that, was when a deer ran out in front of me. That's the first time I've been close to one, and I'd rather not have seen it like that."

Nathan had to smile at that. "You should be thankful you didn't hit it," he said. "If you had, not only would you have got even closer to it, you'd have made a mess of your car."

"That's true. Don't get me wrong," Louisa paused to take a sip of her wine, "I like deer, I think they're beautiful and graceful creatures, but I don't like the way they think it's alright to just run out in front of traffic."

Nathan's smile broadened at that; Louisa made it sound as though deer were not only intelligent enough to know the consequences of running out in front of traffic, but perverse enough to do so, despite the risk, simply to annoy drivers.

"Have you settled in alright?" he asked, changing the subject.

"Sure, it didn't take long. I've been checking the village out, there's not much to it, is there," Louisa remarked.

"It's a village, there isn't supposed to be much to it," Nathan said. "Besides, you're not here for the village, you're here because you want to do a story on the ocelots in the countryside; wildcats and greenery should be of more interest to you than the village."

"That's true. Go on then, tell me about the ocelots, and about this Floyd Mantle who's going to help me with the story."

It didn't take Nathan long to do so, there wasn't much to tell, especially given what he had already told her in his email and on the phone. "I saw Floyd earlier and told him just how interested you are in his wildcats; he's agreed to meet us here later so the two of you can discuss exactly what you want and how to get it.

"He doesn't want paying for his help..."

"That's good." Louisa had no problem with paying people for a story, but she was still working on establishing her website and building her income and couldn't afford to spend a lot of money on a story, at least not when there was no certainty of her making a profit from it.

"But it would be good if you could at least make sure that he's mentioned prominently." Nathan had to lean back out of the way then to give the waiter space to put down his meal. "Floyd told me that although he's studying both zoology and veterinary medicine, he'd rather be a zoologist than a vet, and publishing and publicity really help to get a good position as a zoologist."

"Sure, whatever he wants," Louisa said. "As long as it doesn't interfere with the story, I don't mind giving him a big mention. If he wants, I can always do an interview with him to run alongside the main story: trainee zoologist discovers England's first confirmed wildcats in...however long it's been and is fighting for their right to stay in the home they've established on Dartmoor."

Nathan had to chuckle at that. As always, he was amazed by his friend's ability to take the dry facts of a situation and turn them into something that people were desperate to read. "You haven't even met the guy yet and you're already making him sound like the hero of the zoological world. You'll have everyone believing that he's the next David Attenborough before you're finished."

It was Louisa's turn to laugh. "I doubt that, though if you happen to know how I could get hold of David Attenborough, we could really make this story go global, which would be great for the cats, great for Mr Mantle's career prospects..."

"And great for your website," Nathan finished for his friend when she fell silent, her attention on something going on over his shoulder. Curious, he turned to see what was going on and saw Jennifer Pierson moving amongst the tables, stopping at each in turn to speak to the guests. He couldn't be sure of the reason for what she was doing but based on the consternation and concern he could see on the faces of many of those she spoke to, he could only assume that it had something to do with the death of her mother and the investigation into it.

"I'm very sorry to disturb your meal, Mr Stone," Jennifer Pierson said in a soft voice, crouching at his side when she reached the table where he was eating with Louisa Orchard. She was doing her best to be as unobtrusive as possible, even though she had spoken to the other guests with the same purpose already. "But Constable Havers has asked us to tell all guests that he will be here to speak to you at nine o'clock, so if you're planning on going for a walk or anything after dinner, you need to be back at the hotel for nine."

"Thank you. I'll make sure not to go too far."

"What do you think that's about?" Louisa asked quietly once Jennifer Pierson had moved away from the table. "Do you think it's to do with the investigation you told me about?"

"I can't imagine what else it could be about." Nathan dismissed the matter then and turned his attention back to the food in front of him, which was of more interest to him after his walk to the lake and back.

10

The small restaurant was crowded come nine o'clock. It was filled with guests, staff, and other people who were either there because Constable Havers had requested their presence or because they were curious, but Nathan and Louisa found space at the bar.

Nathan didn't mind being a little cramped for the position afforded him a view of most of the people in the restaurant. He could see the beefy gentleman he had noted that morning, and his wife, almost hidden by her husband's bulk, and the librarian-looking Elizabeth Creek, who wore a pained expression, as though being around so many people in such a confined space was a trying experience for her. Another of the guests caught his eye as well, someone he hadn't previously noted.

The gentleman Nathan's eyes came to rest on, briefly, was slim, almost emaciated, and a little over six feet tall. He was bald and had a smooth, unwrinkled face that made it almost impossible to tell his age. He was wearing jeans and a casual top and gave every indication of being utterly indifferent to being asked to attend a meeting about a death.

None of that was what caught Nathan's eye and made him pay attention to the man, though, what did was the way his eyes roved around the dining room, as though searching for dangers.

He might be dressed casually, like pretty much everyone else in the dining room, but Nathan was sure that the clothes were where any similarity between the man and the other guests at the hotel ended. After years of investigating and arresting criminals, Nathan could tell when he was in the presence of someone who was used to breaking the law, and he was prepared to put money on the man having a lengthy record covering a variety of crimes, including crimes of violence.

Why such a person had chosen a quiet Devonshire village for his holiday, Nathan didn't know, and it made his instincts twitch as he wondered about a possible connection between the man and the dead Tracey Pierson. He could be mistaken, it was possible for career criminals, even those accustomed to violence, to enjoy holidaying in places like Devon, but he was curious.

"Ladies and gentlemen, ladies and gentlemen." Constable Havers' voice climbed until it was loud enough to be heard above the drone of conversation that filled the restaurant.

Nathan craned his head to look past the gentleman next to him at the constable, who was trying hard to make himself visible to everyone. Alongside Havers were David and Jennifer Pierson, both of whom looked miserable. Nathan tried not to read too much into how the Piersons looked, but his experience led him to suspect that the latest news on the situation was that Tracey Pierson had not died of natural causes or as the result of an accident.

"Before I begin, I'd like to apologise, once again, for disturbing your holidays, and your work, for those of you who aren't on holiday," Havers said. "Unfortunately, this morning's incident has become more serious. While it was initially thought that Tracey Pierson's death was an accident, the post-mortem, which took place this afternoon, has revealed that she was murdered."

A chorus of gasps and other expressions of dismay sounded from around the dining room as people reacted to the announcement.

Automatically, Nathan noted those in the room who either remained silent or otherwise reacted in a way that didn't seem right for the circumstances. The Piersons had obviously heard the news already, so their silence was understandable, while the others who failed to react, or at least react as expected, were those he had already marked mentally: Elizabeth Creek appeared overly distressed by the news, which didn't seem right unless she knew Tracey Pierson, though he supposed she could be one of those sensitive people who overreacted to almost everything; the large man, whose name he hadn't picked up, was utterly indifferent to the announcement that had been made — his wife, from what Nathan could see of her, was appropriately upset — as was the thin man, who gave every appearance of hearing that people had died on a regular basis and so was used to it.

One other person caught Nathan's attention because of his reaction to the news of Tracey Pierson's murder. He had only glimpsed the man before then, but he thought he was one of the kitchen workers. The expression on the man's face was that of someone fighting not to reveal how deeply he was distressed by the news; it was clear that he felt a sense of loss at Tracey Pierson's death that went beyond that of an employee for an employer, or even that of someone for a friend.

Nathan suspected that he had found the person who had been out in the woods with Tracey Pierson prior to her death. There was no time for him to reflect on either the discovery of Tracey Pierson's possible lover, or the abnormal reactions of the guests he had noted, for Constable Havers was still speaking.

"Given what the post-mortem has revealed, and I'm sure you understand that I cannot go into details right now, it will be necessary for me to question you all again. It might even be necessary for me to search your rooms." That announcement brought consternation to the faces of many of those crowding the dining room, though Havers showed no sign of being aware of what his words had provoked. "Under the circumstances, I'm afraid it won't be possible for any of you to leave. I apologise for any inconvenience this might cause, but I think you'll agree that if you have to prolong your stay somewhere, this is as good a place as any.

"I promise, as soon as I've made certain that you weren't involved, I will be giving each of you permission to leave."

"Seems like I picked the perfect time to come down to this little slice of heaven," Louisa remarked to Nathan once the clearly out of his depth constable had finished with the gathering in the dining room. "A mysterious group of wildcats, a murder, and a group of guests that can best be described as diverse and suspicious — and that's just based on my first impression of them — and all of that in a scenic setting. If I didn't know better, I'd say we were in an Agatha Christie novel."

"Does that make me Poirot?" Nathan asked.

"Maybe if you put on some weight, grow a moustache, and start using a silly accent," Louisa said. "You could always be Miss Marple instead, all you'd need for that is a sex-change and some hair dye."

"No thanks. I think I'll stick with being me. Besides, it's not like we have to rely on elderly private investigators who just happen to be in the right place at the right time, this is the modern era and we have decent communications and better access to the outside world."

"That's true. How long do you think it'll be before we get a detective here?"

Nathan shrugged. "Realistically, it shouldn't take them any longer than 'til tomorrow morning; they'll have been notified already that this is a murder case, so now it just comes down to which police authority has jurisdiction over the village, and whether they have someone who can be spared from their regular duties." He drained the last of his cider and pushed the glass across the bar for a refill. He was drinking more than he did normally, but he didn't let it bother him, after all, what was the point of taking a holiday if not to relax. "Let's not worry too much about something that is neither in our control nor our problem to worry about. Here comes Floyd Mantle, let's find out what he can do to help you with the ocelot story."

"Sorry I'm so late," Floyd apologised breathlessly as he hurried up to the pair. "I've been with Jennifer, making sure she's alright after the news." The ashen pallor of his face and the shaking of his hands suggested that he had been hit just as hard by the news of what had happened as his friend. Turning to Louisa, he introduced himself, "Hi, Floyd Mantle; I'm guessing you're the friend Nathan told me is interested in writing a story about the ocelots we have around here, Louisa Orchard, right?"

Louisa nodded. "That's right. We can postpone and do this another time, if you'd rather. I know the circumstances aren't great right now." As much as she wanted to get moving on the story, she appreciated that with what was going on the young zoology student might need some time. "I'm booked in for the next three nights, and I can extend that if need be."

"Thanks, but if you want this story any time soon, I don't think it would be a good idea to delay. I take it neither of you has seen the weather report this evening," Floyd said when he saw the curious and confused looks on the faces of the pair before him.

They both shook their heads, but it was Louisa who spoke first, "No, is there's a problem? The weather's looking good as far as I'm aware."

"It was looking good. Unfortunately, that's supposed to change by morning. If the forecast is right, we're going to be hit by a storm during the night: strong winds, heavy rain, perhaps even thunder and lightning. It's supposed to last all through tomorrow and into Friday, if not longer. The rain might even be torrential.

"If you want to see the ocelots, your best bet is to come out with me tonight and hope that they come down to the stream to drink like they usually do."

"I don't mind chancing a bit of wind and rain to get pictures for a story," Louisa said. As annoying as bad weather could be, she found missing out on an important picture or story even more so.

"It'll be more than just a bit of wind and rain," Floyd told her. "Around here storm's get pretty bad. The moors are wide open, so if you're out there there's no escape from the weather. And you're not safe if you're in the village because it's in a valley; too much rain in a short space of time can cause the river to burst its banks. Too bad a storm and the road gets washed out, cutting us off almost completely; it happens several times almost every winter. If it's really bad the village itself might be flooded."

"I don't know why we bother with weather forecasters," Nathan remarked. "They didn't predict the sudden heat we've had the last couple of days, and they don't seem to have predicted this storm ahead of time either."

"Are you trying to tell us," Louisa went on, ignoring Nathan for the moment, "that even without the constable telling us we can't leave until the investigation is over, if we don't leave tonight, it might not be possible for us to leave."

"For the next couple of days at least, yes," Floyd said. "It might not be as bad as they're saying. As Nathan said, the forecasters can't seem to predict anything, but if I were you, I'd take the opportunity to leave before the weather sets in. The other guests don't have the option, they have to be here because of the investigation, but you do."

Louisa thought about it for barely a second before saying, "I'll stick around. If I leave and come back later, I'll have wasted my time and money. Even if the storm is as bad as you say it could be, I'm sure I can find some way of passing the time profitably. At the least, I'll be able to interview you and get down everything you know about the ocelots, and I can start work on the story. Is there any chance of getting out there to see the ocelots before the storm hits?"

"Yes, though it could be close." Floyd nodded, glad to have something to think about and focus on other than the death — murder — of his friend's mother. "The storm's not due for several hours yet, but as Nathan can tell you, it's about an hour's walk, longer because we have to go around where the police have got cordoned off, to where we're most likely to see the ocelots, and we might have to wait around for them, assuming they turn up. I hope you've got some good walking shoes, and clothes suitable for less than perfect weather," he said. "Even if we're lucky enough to get there and back before the storm hits, we'll still need warm clothes that'll protect us against both the cold and the plant life that's likely to try and scratch us to pieces."

"I'm sure I can come up with something suitable," Louisa said confidently.

11

Louisa shivered, despite the layers of t-shirt, jumper and jacket she was wearing, and stripped the excess water from her face with her hand.

The gesture was automatic, she was far too soaked for it to make any real difference to her, as was Nathan, who squelched up the stairs at her side. Together they resembled a pair of oversized, half-drowned rats.

The storm that Floyd Mantle had warned them about had held off until they were on their way back from ocelot-spotting. It was just as well it had for the fifteen or so minutes they were out in it was more than long enough to leave them thoroughly drenched and very uncomfortable.

Despite their current physical situation, they were both happy for all three ocelots had come down to the small, stream-fed pool that seemed to be their favoured watering hole. Not only had they managed to get photographs and video of all three drinking together from the pool, they had been only a dozen feet away when the ocelots left to return to wherever it was they had their lair.

"How much do you think proper video equipment would cost?" Louisa asked as they reached the second-floor landing, where they were to part company, she to head along the passage to her room and Nathan to carry on up to the next floor, where his room was. "The sort used by wildlife documentary-makers, the sort with top quality infra-red and night vision capability."

"More than you can afford," Nathan said. Expensive was as close a guess as he could make, he didn't have the first clue what sort of price might be attached to such a piece of equipment, only that it wouldn't be cheap. "You're not thinking of turning documentary filmmaker, are you? Because, no offence, I think you're better off sticking to journalism."

Louisa gave a disappointed sigh. "I guess you're right. It'd be nice to have some better-quality footage to go with the article I'm going to write, though. What you got last night, and what I got tonight, is alright, good enough for my website, but I know I could do so much better with the right equipment."

"I'm sure you're right. You'll just have to make do with what you've got, though. After all, nobody's going to expect David Attenborough level film quality from a news website. Besides, what you have is good enough for people to know the footage is genuine. Anyway, I really need to get some sleep, so I'll see you in the morning." With that Nathan headed up the stairs to the next floor while Louisa made her way along the passage.

Nathan yawned as he walked down the third-floor passage. He was looking forward to getting into bed, he was even more tired than he had been last night after seeing the ocelots, but sleep was pushed from his mind when he approached the door to his room. The door was ajar, and a thin sliver of light shone through it to illuminate a part of the wall opposite.

He was certain that he hadn't left his room open when he left, which meant someone had broken in, and the only reason he could think of for someone to do that was to rob him. It wasn't the first time he had been a victim of a crime, but it was the first time he had been robbed, if that was what was happening. He supposed it was his perverse sense of humour, but it amused him that it had happened when he was on holiday and had little of value with him, and most of what he did have was on his person.

As stealthily as he could in his sodden clothes, Nathan made his way along the passage. He considered calling the police, or going for help, but quickly decided against doing either; with the weather worsening there was every chance that the police wouldn't be able to get there, at least not without a major delay, and he didn't think it appropriate to ask anyone else to risk themselves in checking his room with him.

The intruder was doing their best to be quiet, but Nathan could hear them moving about as he got closer. It was hard to tell what they were doing but it didn't matter, what did was that they were in his room without permission.

As silent as he endeavoured to be, Nathan wasn't silent enough. He was half a dozen feet from the door of his room when he was betrayed by the hotel — a floorboard creaked under his foot. The noise of the storm should have drowned the squeak but somehow it didn't, the high pitch of the floorboard seemed to cut through the howling of the wind to alert the person in his room.

Nathan reached the door of his room in time for it to be thrown open as the intruder made their escape. Something solid struck him on the side of the head, knocking him sideways and sending him to the floor, where he saw stars. Through his dizziness he saw the back of a person, unidentifiable thanks to a long, dark coat, he couldn't even tell their sex, running down the passage towards the stairs.

Slowly, Nathan pushed himself to his feet, swallowing against the nausea that left an unpleasant taste in his mouth. He leant against the wall to stay upright and cautiously shook his head to clear the dizziness while he debated whether to give chase or to check his room to see what, if anything, had been taken.

By the time he had cleared his head sufficiently to make movement a safe proposition the figure was out of sight. That made up his mind for him; since there was no way for him to know where the intruder was headed, giving chase would be a pointless waste of his time. Whoever had hit him could disappear into any room, or even leave the hotel and disappear into the storm.

Entering his room Nathan found it in disarray. The wardrobe doors were ajar, kept from closing by his clothes, most of which had been pulled from the hangars, and in some cases torn in the process; his bags had been searched and the small amount they had held scattered across the bed and floor; the bed was messy, as though the intruder had searched it for anything that might have been hidden between the sheets or under the mattress, and the drawers of the small bedside cabinet stood open, though there had been little in them to be rifled through.

As far as he could tell, the only thing missing from his room was the only thing of value that had been there, his laptop. That wasn't much of a loss in his opinion for all his important files, mostly just pictures and video clips of his wife and kids, were backed up online thanks to his sister, who understood computers better than he did.

Once he had finished his brief examination of the room Nathan returned to the passage, where he took out his phone.

12

"Are you sure your laptop is the only thing that was taken?" Havers asked from where he stood in the doorway of Nathan's room, his eyes on the mess that had been left by the intruder.

"As sure as I can be," Nathan said, stifling yet another yawn. It was gone half past two in the morning and he was past ready for bed; his tiredness was made worse by the fact that he was still wearing the soaking clothes he had returned to the hotel in. The dampness had seeped into his muscles, leaving him clammy and uncomfortable, and in need of a hot shower before bed. "It's hard to be certain with everything in a mess, but I am sure that if they took anything other than the laptop, it wasn't worth the effort. I didn't bring much with me, and almost nothing of value; the only things that might be worth taking are my wallet, watch, and my mobile, all of which I have with me."

"So, you think this was just an opportunistic thief who happened to get lucky enough to find you gone from your room after midnight, but unlucky enough not to find much worth stealing?" The doubt in Havers' voice made it clear that he believed there was more going on than what he had been told.

Nathan shrugged. "I realise it doesn't sound very likely, but I don't know what else I can tell you. Going out wasn't a spur of the moment thing, but it was organised late, so it's not as though someone could have planned the break-in, not in any great detail anyway." He shifted about, plucking at his clothes, pulling them away from his clammy skin as he tried to make himself less uncomfortable. "All I can think is that the person who broke in here overheard the conversation in which I said I would be out tonight and decided to take advantage of the opportunity."

"As I understand it, from what you have told me so far, Mr Stone, your conversation would have revealed that your friend..." Havers had to consult the notes he had taken. "Ms Orchard would also be out of her room. Why did this intruder target you and not her?"

"How am I supposed to know that?" Tiredness and discomfort combined to make Nathan terser than he would normally have been. "Maybe the burglar saw me with my laptop at some point and decided it meant I've got stuff worth taking, or maybe they didn't know which room was Louisa's, or maybe they already tried Louisa's room and found nothing worth taking." Even as he said it Nathan knew how unlikely that was; Louisa had taken both her cameras, the still and the video, into the woods on their ocelot hunt but that still left her laptop and tablet, and whatever else she had brought with her.

"Or perhaps you have something to hide concerning the murder of Tracey Pierson, and you're trying to conceal it by inventing this supposed burglar who broke into your room and messed everything up but only stole one thing."

Nathan could only stare at the constable in disbelief. More than a minute and a half passed, during which he struggled to unstick his dumbstruck mind, before he was able to respond. "Why on earth would you think that?" he asked. "Even assuming I was, somehow, involved in her death, which I wasn't, what good would it do to fake a break-in and theft of my laptop? Doing so wouldn't conceal anything, nor would it divert attention from me. All it would do is put more attention onto me." He did his best to make a logical and lucid argument, but it quickly became clear that he was wasting his time; Havers had latched onto the idea like a dog with a bone, and he wasn't about to let go.

"Perhaps there's something on the laptop that would prove your connection to Tracey Pierson and her murder," Havers said. "When you heard me say that I'll be searching everyone's rooms, you realised you had to prevent me checking your laptop and discovering what's on it. You couldn't just hide it or dispose of it, too many people have seen you with it. What better way to get rid of the laptop, without seeming to be responsible yourself, than to fake a break-in?"

"And I suppose I hit myself round the head," Nathan said with thinly veiled sarcasm as he pointed to the lump raised on the side of his head.

Havers shrugged. "If you're capable of murder, I don't see why you wouldn't have injured yourself to make your story more believable. What I can't understand is why you think I'd accept the notion that a burglar, one who knows you're going to be away from the hotel for some time, would wait to break into your room until you were returning to it. That simply doesn't make sense. And, under the circumstances, I'm going to have to make your room the first I search."

To say that Nathan was stunned was an understatement. He could think of only one occasion to match what he was feeling, and he was hard-pressed to say which occasion surprised him more: being told that his wife and children had died because of an arson attack or being accused of murder. He supposed they were about even in the level of surprise they inspired, it was just that the surprise was different in each case.

He had no chance to react. Before he could recover enough to think of a response, let alone utter it, Havers spoke again.

"Nathan Stone, I am placing you under arrest on suspicion of the murder of Tracey Pierson, you do not have to say anything..."

Nathan's surprise increased. He wanted to tell the constable that he was a detective inspector and make it clear what a huge mistake he was making, but he couldn't form the words. All he could do was stand there dumbly as the idiot constable finished reading him his rights and then handcuffed him, doing so with a roughness that reminded him of the many times criminals had complained when he handcuffed them. He couldn't help thinking that there might have been some validity to their complaints, not that the thought did him much good just then.

ONCE HE RECOVERED HIS voice, which took him the better part of a quarter of an hour, Nathan attempted to get the constable to listen to him. Havers showed no interest in what his suspect had to say, though; all he did seem bothered about was keeping away the curious holidaymakers who filled the passage after having their sleep disturbed and searching Nathan's room, with the help of his fellow constable, Fulton, who was hastily summoned to the hotel despite being on holiday, a holiday he was spending at home.

If things had been bad for Nathan before, they became a whole lot worse when Havers emerged from the room, a triumphant look on his face and a bloodstained meat tenderiser in a clear plastic evidence bag.

"Would you care to explain how this came to be in your belongings?" Havers asked, holding the evidence bag up accusingly.

COLD, WET, HUNGRY, thirsty, and above all else irritable, Nathan sat in a less than comfortable seat in Donningford's small police station while Havers went through the process of booking him in. It was a process that seemed to take far longer than usual, something he felt could be put down to the fact that he was on the opposite side of the process to that which he was accustomed to.

"Name?" Havers asked brusquely.

"Nathan Stone." He smiled as he said, "Detective Inspector Nathan Stone of Branton CID." He took a perverse delight in seeing Havers' jaw drop in stunned dismay.

"Can...can you prove that?" Havers asked in a voice that wobbled far more than he liked.

"If you'll take the cuffs off." Nathan wasn't best pleased that the handcuffs had been left on him for so long.

Nathan rubbed at his wrists, which had been chafed by the cold metal of the handcuffs, until he had regained all the feeling he suspected he was going to get. Only then did he reach into his pocket for his wallet. He opened it to reveal his warrant card, which he had long ago become accustomed to carrying with him wherever he went, even when he was off-duty or on holiday. He held it out for inspection by Havers, who scrutinised it carefully with a growing look of dismay as it became clear that the card was real.

"I'm very sorry for the mix-up, sir," Havers said quickly. "It was an honest mistake, I'm sure you can see that."

Nathan said nothing, he simply allowed Havers' embarrassment to grow while he struggled to properly apologise for his mistake.

AFTER NEARLY FORTY minutes, by which time it was almost a quarter to four, Nathan had dealt with most of his problems; he was no longer either hungry or thirsty, and he was no longer cold, but he was still tired and irritable.

He wanted nothing more than to go back to the hotel and crawl into bed, so he could sleep for about twelve hours. That was not possible, however, for there was the question of the bloodstained meat tenderiser found amongst his ransacked belongings to be dealt with — it had been discovered under the clothes at the bottom of the wardrobe.

"So, you can't provide any description for the person who broke into your room, stole your laptop, and hid the tenderiser?" Havers asked, wanting clarification of what he had been told already.

Nathan shook his head, an action he regretted immediately for the blow he had received had left him with a headache. "They were maybe five-nine, perhaps a bit shorter, and slim to medium in build. That's all I can tell you," he said after a moment's reflection, during which he tried to dredge up any details he might have noticed without realising. Nothing came to mind. "They were wearing a long, dark overcoat of some sort, and something over their head, I don't know what. The passage was dark, and I only got a brief glimpse of them through the stars I was seeing after they hit me. I can't even tell you if they were male or female, though if pressed I'd say it was a bloke, based on how easily they floored me." He didn't need the look from Havers to know that there was every chance his mind was rejecting the possibility of his assailant being female simply because he didn't like the thought that he had been floored by someone of the supposedly weaker sex.

"It's not much to go on," Havers said needlessly. "Can you think why Tracey Pierson's murderer would have tried to frame you? Or why they would have made such an obvious mess while doing so? It doesn't many any sense. Why even try to make it look like they had robbed you; surely that ran the risk of you discovering the murder weapon — we won't know for certain until the tenderiser has been tested, but I think it's safe to assume that it is the murder weapon — while looking to see what was missing, which would give you a chance to get rid of it before it could get you into trouble.

"It's only because you didn't search the room, I did, that you ended up being suspected, if only for a while."

Nathan chose not to point out that Havers had only searched his room because he had already leapt to the conclusion that he was involved with the murder. Finding the tenderiser had only helped the constable to decide that he was right.

"I can't say why they tried to frame me, I have no connection to Mrs Pierson, or any of the family," Nathan said. "All I can think is that they must have somehow discovered that I was in the woods last night, and that I saw Mrs Pierson while on my way back to the hotel. As for the supposed burglary, that was actually pretty clever, and might well have worked as they probably wanted it to if I wasn't a detective. I can only surmise what their thinking was, but I imagine they believed that if I saw the room had been burgled, I would immediately make a search to see what was missing, as most people would, and in doing so I would have found the tenderiser. A regular person would have picked up the tenderiser the moment they found it, out of curiosity if nothing else, and put their fingerprints on it, making it that much harder to convince anyone that they weren't the killer.

"If the tenderiser had been hidden and the room not been made to look as though it had been burgled they wouldn't have been able to get my prints on it."

"You're saying we're looking for a clever killer?" Havers asked.

Nathan shrugged tiredly. He didn't know enough about the case to be able to answer that question, and curious as he was he wasn't sure he wanted to know. It wasn't his case and it wasn't his jurisdiction, so the best thing he could do was keep his involvement with it as minimal as possible. Not that that was seeming to be easy to manage so far since bad luck, or some higher power, had him in the thick of the investigation.

13

The distant ringing of a bell intruded on Nathan's sleep, nudging him towards consciousness. It seemed to take a long time for him to wake, and it was only when his fog-filled brain registered that the bell he could hear was the ringing of his phone that he came fully awake.

He groaned in dismay at having his sleep, sorely needed after his later than expected night, disturbed and forced his eyes open as he groped for his phone. He found it and got it to his ear long before he managed to unglue his eyes, not that opening them made any difference for no light came through the curtains covering the window.

"Stone," he croaked into the phone. He hoped that the roughness of his voice stemmed from a lack of sleep and didn't herald the onset of a cold, brought on by getting drenched, being forced to spend too long in his sodden clothes, and then getting soaked again after changing. His holiday had already suffered enough, without it being threatened by the possibility of illness.

"You sound bloody awful, Nathan."

"Thank you, sir." That was the last thing Nathan wanted to hear from his superior, but he supposed he should have expected some remark, given how bad he sounded to his own ears. "To what do I owe the pleasure of a call from you on my holiday?" Now that he could make out the room's contents well enough to see what he was doing he pushed himself into a seated position and reached for the glass on the bedside cabinet. He hoped that some water would clear the croakiness from his voice.

Nathan was friendly with his superior, Detective Chief Inspector Collins, but not to the extent that it was anything other than unusual for him to call while he was on holiday. Only something important could have prompted the call, and Nathan had to admit to being curious, though he realised there was a good chance he wouldn't get to find out what it was. The storm outside had become much stronger since he made it back to the hotel and it was interfering with the already poor signal his phone got in Donningford.

"I'm sorry, sir, you're going to have to repeat that," Nathan said as his superior's voice was cut off by a burst of static that made him yank the phone from his ear to avoid his hearing being damaged. "The signal's really poor."

"...to the point," Collins said, speaking quickly to try and get his message across before the weather could interrupt again. "And send you an email with the details." Another burst of static cut off the beginning of what he said next. "...you're mixed up in down there by the assistant chief constable for Devon; he called me at home first thing, ...to know about you."

Nathan did his best to make sense of the gaps in what his superior was saying. If he was right, and he wouldn't have liked to wager any serious money on it, then Collins knew about the murder of Tracey Pierson and that he was unwittingly mixed up in it. The assistant chief constable for Devon had called Collins to tell him about the involvement of one of his officers, and to find out about said officer.

It was strange for an assistant chief constable to get involved in a relatively simple murder case, but not entirely unheard of, especially when the murder investigation included a detective inspector among the suspects.

He felt a strange sense of foreboding as he listened to the rest of what his superior had to say.

"I assured him you wouldn't have been involved in the murder. Potter believed me because he wants you to take...the investigation. The storm you've got going on down there...can't get a detective out to the village for at least a day, it's too...Think you can manage?"

"The ACC for Devon wants me to take charge of the investigation because he can't get a detective out here because of the storm?" Nathan asked, wanting clarification of what he had put together from the garbled phone call.

"Are you okay with that?" Collins asked. "You can...if you want, you are on holiday, ...situation is complicated."

Complicated was something of an understatement, Nathan thought; he was possibly the last person, barring the murderer, to have seen Tracey Pierson alive, and the murder weapon had been found in his room. Common-sense suggested that the best thing he could do was have as little to do with the investigation as possible.

It was some comfort to know that he couldn't be forced to take on the investigation, both because he was on holiday and because he didn't work for the Devonshire constabulary. Nonetheless, he knew it would not be a good idea for him to deny a request from an assistant chief constable, regardless of the circumstances.

"I'll do it," he said, throwing back the covers so he could get to his feet.

"...on your emails, I'll send...details on what..."

The interference from the weather picked up, garbling about half of what Collins said that time, before finally getting so bad that the signal disappeared completely, ending the call.

With the phone call over, thanks to the weather, Nathan returned the phone to the bedside cabinet. He wasted no time in getting dressed in the clothes reluctantly loaned him by Constable Havers, which had thankfully dried off after getting drenched on the way back to the hotel from the police station, and within a couple of minutes he was on his way down the passage to the stairs.

Many people would have been annoyed to have their holiday cut short, but not Nathan. While he would have preferred to continue his holiday, the weather was so horrible that he was glad to have something to do other than sit around the hotel, hoping that the weather would improve.

Less than ten minutes after the abrupt end to his phone call, Nathan was at the door of Louisa's room on the second floor. It was yet to reach half past nine, which meant his friend was most likely still in bed, since she wouldn't have got to sleep much before three — he didn't like to think about how late it had been when he managed to get to bed, in a different room to the one he had been given when he arrived now that that was a crime scene.

Ordinarily he wouldn't have disturbed his friend, he might have to deal with a lack of sleep but that didn't mean Louisa should too, but with his laptop missing he needed her help to access his emails.

Louisa opened the door to her room abruptly, a blistering insult on her lips, ready to be unleashed on the person foolish enough to have disturbed her sleep. She swallowed the insult when she saw who was responsible for disturbing her, though she couldn't entirely keep the annoyance she felt from her voice.

"I hope there's a really good reason for this, Nate," she said curtly. "That storm's making it hard enough to sleep without you getting in on the act."

"Sorry, Lou, I'd've let you sleep but I have got a good reason for waking you, trust me," Nathan said apologetically. "I need to borrow your laptop."

"My laptop? Why, what's up? What's wrong with yours?" Surprise chased sleep from Louisa's mind, though it didn't rid her of her confusion.

"It's been stolen. It's a long story, and one I'm sure you'll be very interested in," Nathan told his friend. "I'll explain it all to you, just as soon as there's a chance. Right now, though, I need your laptop. I need to check my emails, I'm expecting something important."

"Stolen?" Other questions, *'how, why, when'* rose to her lips but went no further, now wasn't the time for them, Louisa realised. "Sure, come in." She swung the door wide to make space for Nathan to enter the room and then closed it behind him. Two steps brought her to the bed and bending down she pulled her laptop out, so she could turn it on.

"Here you go," she said once it had booted up and she had logged on.

"Thanks." Nathan accepted the laptop and took a seat on the bed next to Louisa. He blinked in surprise when he looked at the screen; the desktop was cluttered with numerous icons for programs and files, much more than he was used to dealing with, and it took him a while to find the one he was after.

Louisa rested a hand on Nathan's shoulder and her chin on the back of that hand as she watched what he was doing. She wasn't concerned that he was going to do anything that would damage her laptop, though she knew he was far from confident when it came to electronic devices and prone to creating problems, she was merely curious.

It took Nathan almost five minutes to connect to the internet, log out of Louisa's email account and log in to his own, a length of time that had Louisa cursing the storm, and which tried Nathan's patience and reminded him of why he was not a fan of technology. Every time he thought he had succeeded in logging in, he got a message telling him there was no connection and he had to try again.

When he did, finally, manage to access his email account he quickly opened the message from his superior, while mentally crossing his fingers that the connection would remain stable long enough for him to read it.

"What the hell?" Louisa exclaimed, reading the email over Nathan's shoulder. "They found the murder weapon in your room? I think you'd better tell me what's been going on since I left you last night." She shifted her position on the bed, so she could better see Nathan, who turned to face her. "The last thing I heard, that Constable Havers was declaring the death a murder. Since then the murder weapon's been found in your room, and the assistant chief constable for Devon has requested that you take over the investigation? I don't get it, it doesn't make sense."

It took Nathan a short while to explain all that had transpired since the two of them separated on the stairs during the night. Like Louisa, he had a hard time understanding how he had become prime suspect, and then gone from prime suspect to lead investigator so quickly, the latter solely because he was a detective inspector and the storm outside prevented any other detective reaching the village.

Of the two positions, he knew which he preferred. It was far better to be the one doing the investigating than to be the one being investigated.

14

Havers, a look of almost scared nervousness on his face, stood before the desk in the manager's office of The Moor's Edge hotel. His uniform was soaked through, despite him having been outside for only as long as it took to get from his front door to his car and from his car to the hotel foyer, but he didn't dare make a move to try and ease his discomfort.

As glad as he was to have someone else in charge of the murder investigation, he wasn't sure how to feel about the investigation being put in the hands of someone who, however briefly, had been a suspect.

"I realise you're probably not all that happy that I've been put in charge of this case," Nathan said from his seat on the other side of the desk.

"Not at all, sir," Havers lied. "I'm glad to have you in charge of this case." *Instead of me.*

Nathan didn't need to hear the unspoken end to the constable's sentence to know what it was. "Since I'm coming to this case late, I'm at a bit of a disadvantage, so what I need from you is a copy of everything you have so far: post-mortem report, scene-of-crime report, and any notes you've taken, as well as everything you have on the interviews you've conducted. Once I've had a chance to go through all of that, I'll want to speak to you and get your impressions on everything."

"Yes, sir, I'll get the files." Havers left without another word.

IT TOOK NATHAN MORE than three hours and half a dozen cups of coffee, as well as the largest fried breakfast he could remember seeing let alone eating, to get through everything that was in the case file for Tracey Pierson's murder, and to get Constable Havers' opinions on the people questioned so far.

The complexity of the case was not what had taken him so long, there was little in the way of complexity about it, other than the attempt to frame him by planting the murder weapon in his room. It was the wealth of information, much of it unnecessary, that Havers had seen fit to put in the file.

Nathan had seen it before with officers who had little to no experience with major investigations; they were so afraid of omitting something important that they included everything, regardless of its relevance.

"Given that they can't even get a detective here, because of the storm," Nathan said, "I think it's safe to say that it will be tomorrow at the earliest before we can get a forensics team here."

"Actually, sir," Havers spoke up hesitantly. "The forensics team have already been."

"Why isn't there anything in here from them then?" Nathan asked, gesturing to the file in front of him.

"Because we haven't received anything from them yet," Havers told him. "They said it would be today at the earliest, and probably tomorrow, if not longer, before they'd have any results from their tests, and even that would be limited. They did a preliminary examination of the area where Tracey Pierson's body was found, but said they'd have to come back and do a more thorough job. They intended coming back today."

"Obviously that's had to be cancelled because of the weather." Nathan was pleased that a forensic examination of the area where the body was found had been made, it meant things weren't quite as bad as he had initially thought, but he was all too aware of how much the weather was going to hamper his investigation.

The storm outside was raging far too fiercely for him to even consider making a trip out into the woods to examine the crime scene, which, according to the crudely drawn map included in the file, was only a stone's throw from where he had seen Tracey Pierson, and only a stone's throw from the river. By the time it was safe for him to go out there, the crime scene would most likely have been destroyed by the weather, which meant all he could do was hope that the forensics team had already found whatever there was to be discovered, or that it would somehow survive the storm.

"Yes, sir. I wasn't able to get hold of the forensics team myself, the weather is causing havoc with our ability to communicate with the outside world, but when I spoke to my superior he told me they will be here as soon as the weather clears and the road into the village is passable. A detective will be sent to take over the case at that time as well, assuming you haven't solved it by then."

Nathan wasn't sure how he should take that remark, so he ignored it. "How long after the weather clears before the road's likely to be passable?" Though he had heard and read of villages being cut off by severe storms, he found it hard to believe, now that he was in such a position, that it could happen in a supposedly modern country.

"That's hard to say, sir," Havers said. "This storm is out of season; normally we don't get one this strong until mid-winter, and then we're generally somewhere near the bottom of the list when it comes to being rescued. Usually it's days, if not a week or more, before the road gets re-opened, but that's mostly because it's just the villagers being inconvenienced. I'm sure with holidaymakers stuck here, not to mention a murderer on the loose, they'll be quicker about clearing the road." He caught the hard look directed at him by the inspector and swallowed the nervous lump that threatened to close his throat. "Based on past storms, it'll take them a couple of days, once they get to work on it, to clear the road. It all depends on how bad the storm is and what kind of mess it makes."

"So, we're stuck here without help for at least three days, and for at least the next day we can't even count on being able to call anyone to get information. I assume that if people can't get into the village, no-one can get out either."

Havers nodded. "A person could use a boat and get out of the village by the river, but they'd have to be crazy to risk it. With a storm this bad, the river's going to be running high and fast, with a lot of dangers hidden just under the surface. Given how bad it is, you're not just stuck in the village, you're stuck in the hotel. It was all I could do to get here from the station with the case file. I don't plan on leaving again until the storm's over."

"Okay, so we're stuck here with the killer. Lou was right, this is an Agatha Christie novel," Nathan said aloud, though he was speaking to himself rather than to Havers. That wasn't good news as far as Nathan was concerned. If they realised they were trapped for the foreseeable future, there was no telling what the murderer might do, especially if they thought the police were closing in.

Havers didn't understand what the inspector meant; he knew who Agatha Christie was, but what she had to do with the case, he couldn't imagine. He put it from his mind, sure that if it was relevant or important he would be told what it meant, and asked, "What makes you think the killer is still here? They could have left after killing Mrs Pierson."

Nathan shook his head. "If they left after the murder, who was it that broke into my room and planted the murder weapon? Besides, whether the murderer we're looking for is one of your villagers, or one of my fellow holidaymakers, their absence would have been noticed by now and suspicion would have fallen on them. Sticking around and acting normally is the best thing the murderer could do."

"But two couples left yesterday, isn't it possible that one of them is the murderer?"

"Possible," Nathan agreed, "but unlikely, because of the attempt to frame me. No-one but the murderer is going to have done that." He frowned, there was something niggling at the back of his mind, something in what he had read, but he couldn't tease it to the front where he could grab hold of it and determine its importance. "You might as well go and get yourself something to eat, I want to read through this lot again." He smiled briefly. "I'd tell you to be back within the hour, but since you can't leave the hotel without putting your life at risk, you won't be going far."

"No, sir. I don't plan on even getting close to the windows, let alone the doors," Havers said. "The thunder and lightning were almost directly overhead when I got here."

It took Nathan a while to go back through the files on his commandeered desk, and he managed to get through another coffee before he found what he was looking for. He then went in search of confirmation that he was right.

15

"Mr Pierson, I'm sorry to trouble you at this difficult time, but I need to ask you a few questions."

"It's Mr Stone, isn't it?"

"It's Inspector Stone, actually," Nathan corrected him. "Detective Inspector Nathan Stone. I believe Constable Havers told you earlier that I have been asked to take charge of the investigation into your wife's murder, though, under the circumstances, I can understand why that may have slipped your mind. The situation here is far from ideal, thanks to the weather, but it's because of the weather that I've been asked to take charge. They can't get a detective from a local station so the powers that be have decided to take advantage of the fact that I happened to pick this place for my holiday.

"Now, to get back to where I came in, I have a few questions I hope you won't mind answering."

"Ask whatever you need to," David Pierson said in a voice that made it clear he was past caring about many things, including being asked questions.

"Thank you. Firstly, can you tell me if I am right in thinking that your wife owned a green and blue jacket, with a stain or mark of some kind on the left sleeve?"

Pierson had to think about that for almost a full minute. "Yes, paint got spilt on it during some redecoration work, why?"

Nathan didn't respond, instead he posed another question. "Do you know where the jacket is now?"

A shrug. "It should be in the hall closet, with the rest of the family's jackets," Pierson said, his grief overshadowing and subduing his curiosity, to the point where it showed as no more than a faint glimmer in the recesses of one eye.

"Do you mind if we have a look and see if it's there?"

"HERE IT IS," PIERSON said when he found the jacket in the hall closet of the house, connected to the rear of the hotel, where his family lived. He held out the jacket for the two police officers to see. "Why are you interested in it?" he asked in a monotone that suggested the question was posed automatically rather than out of any curiosity.

"Your wife was wearing the jacket when I saw her in the woods, the night she was killed," Nathan told him. "It wasn't included in the list of things found on or near the body, though. Given that it wasn't very warm out there in the woods, I couldn't imagine why your wife would have taken the jacket off. The absence suggested to me that she was killed somewhere other than where her body was found. It could have been that she was killed in another part of the woods and dumped where she was found." He winced at how callously he had phrased that, but to his relief David Pierson showed no reaction. "But the missing jacket, combined with the choice of murder weapon, which the killer thoughtfully tried to plant in my room, made me think she came home before she was killed."

"I don't understand," Constable Havers said, his brow furrowed as he tried to fathom his way through what Nathan had said.

"It's simple really. Very few people are likely to carry a meat tenderiser with them to a murder," Nathan said. "It's not an ideal weapon to kill someone with, nor is it much of a weapon to take with you if you feel a need to defend yourself. A knife is a much better choice in either case. On the other hand, if you happen to be arguing with someone in a kitchen and they turn their back on you, it's exactly the kind of thing you might snatch up to hit them with.

"There's every chance that a single blow from an angry person could make a murder weapon of even a tenderiser."

"You think Tracey came home before she...before she was killed?" Pierson asked. Something that might have, under other circumstances, passed for interest and curiosity flitted across his face for the briefest of moments.

Nathan nodded. The jacket and the tenderiser were not proof positive, but in the absence of contradictory evidence, it was enough to convince him that Tracey Pierson had been killed either at home or at the hotel. That made it likely that the murderer was someone at the hotel, though whether it was a family member, a member of staff, or a guest remained uncertain.

"Yes, I do. I think she came home, took off the jacket and hung it up in the closet, and then had an argument with someone. An argument which ended with your wife being hit on the head with the tenderiser." Nathan watched David Pierson closely as he said that, searching for anything that might be out of character for a grieving husband. "Whether that blow was intended to kill, or even if any thought was given to the level of damage being inflicted, I can't say at this time. I do feel reasonably confident in saying that the attack on your wife, Mr Pierson, was an impulse action, something done on the spur of the moment, rather than something planned."

The look on Pierson's face made it plain that he was far from pleased to hear that his wife's death was most likely unintended. That didn't really surprise Nathan, but given the questions he had yet to ask, and the reactions they were likely to produce, it was of small importance.

"Did you know your wife was having an affair?" Nathan asked the question baldly, with no attempt to sugarcoat it, as he would have if

Jennifer Pierson had been there, in the hope that the abruptness of the question would provoke an honest answer, or at least make Pierson give away the truth despite whatever he might say.

"Having what? Having an affair? Don't be ridiculous. What...what makes you think Tracey was having an affair?"

Nathan didn't answer straightaway, he was too busy trying to decide if Pierson's denials were genuine. His friend, and occasional partner, DS Stephen Burke would have had no problem; having studied psychology at university, Stephen was skilled at reading body-language and facial expressions, whereas he had to rely on his experience and instinct, neither of which was as trustworthy as he would have liked.

"I encountered your wife in the woods while walking back to the hotel from a rather special encounter with some of your local wildlife. I didn't see her straightaway, she was around a bend in the path from me and out of sight, but I could hear her. Your wife was in conversation with someone, I don't know who, and it is that conversation which leads me to believe that she was having an affair," Nathan said. "Are you telling me that you didn't know about your wife's affair?"

"Of course not. I don't believe she was having one. Tracey would never have cheated on me," Pierson declared, his voice rising in anger. "You must have misheard, either that or you're lying."

"Why would you think I'm lying?" Nathan asked. "I don't know either you or your wife, so I have absolutely no reason for doing so. The conversation I overheard made it pretty clear that your wife was involved with someone other than yourself."

"You're lying!" Pierson came to life, his anger pushing aside his grief for a time.

"In the conversation I overheard, it was also brought up that you have a temper, and that you have in the past, and even recently, struck your wife."

"I've never..." Pierson seemed to realise that his raised voice was doing him no favours for he stopped and fought to get himself under control. "I've never hit Tracey, never. I wouldn't do that, I love her, she's my whole life."

"So says every man convicted of spousal abuse," Nathan remarked, unconvinced by David Pierson's protestations of innocence. He had heard it all before, far too often, from those who claimed they would never hit a woman, least of all their beloved wife or lover. "If you didn't hit your wife, how do you explain this?" From the file he was carrying he took a photograph, one of the many that formed the visual portion of the post-mortem report, and passed it over for Pierson to look at.

"Musta been done by her...by the...by the person who killed her," Pierson said when he found his voice. He couldn't take his eyes off the photograph in his hands, a close-up of his wife's face, pale in death but for where the skin was marred by a bruise. Death had stopped the bruise reaching its full development, but there had still been time for the eye to swell and close and for the skin to darken on its way to the black that signalled a bruise at its peak.

"That's possible," Nathan agreed, "but unlikely. According to the report from the pathologist who carried out the post-mortem, this bruise is older than the injury that killed your wife. She received the bruise somewhere in the region of three to six hours before she died, which means that while it isn't out of the question that she got it at the hands of her killer, it didn't happen at the same time. The pathologist also noted that Mrs Pierson had numerous older injuries. Injuries that had healed, but which were sustained over a prolonged period of time; injuries of a sort commonly found on victims of a domestic abuse: broken bones and scarring on the internal organs.

"Do you still claim not to have a temper, and never to have hit your wife?" Nathan asked. "No, don't bother to deny it, Mr Pierson, I think we can all see that you do have a temper, one that you can't control. It would be best if you start telling the truth; were you responsible for your wife's black eye?"

Pierson ground his teeth and flushed nastily as he fought to control his anger before finally blurting out, "It was her own fault, she should know not to get me upset."

It didn't surprise Nathan that that was what Pierson said. In his experience, those who didn't deny the abuse they inflicted tended to blame their victims for driving them to it. "Why did you hit your wife?" he asked. "Were the two of you arguing?"

Pierson nodded, a single abrupt dip of his head, as though he wanted to get the admission over with as quickly as possible.

"Were you arguing about her affair?"

If the strength of an action was any indication of the validity of the sentiment being expressed, then the rapid and violent shaking of Pierson's head would have convinced even the most hardened of doubters. In case the action wasn't enough, he also denied the cause of the argument between him and his wife vocally, with as much vehemence as he could muster.

"No. I swear! It had nothing to do with that." His hand twitched, as though he was about to cross his heart in a gesture of faithfulness. "I swear. If Tracey was having an affair, I knew nothing about it. Maybe Jenny did, but I definitely didn't. Don't you think if I'd killed Tracey because she was having an affair, I'd've killed the guy she was sleeping with as well?"

Nathan had to admit that that did have a ring of truth to it, though he quickly reminded himself that since they didn't know who the other party in the affair was, there was every chance he had been killed and his body awaited discovery. On the other hand, it might be that Pierson hadn't had an opportunity to kill his wife's lover, and was waiting for a chance to do so, perhaps when the investigation into his wife's murder was over and he was in the clear.

"What were you arguing about then, Mr Pierson?" Nathan asked. "I wouldn't have thought it necessary for me to tell you that every time you hesitate to answer one of my questions, and every time I catch you lying to me, it makes me more inclined to believe that you killed your wife and dumped her body in the woods, perhaps hoping that she would roll into the river — she was found only a stone's throw from it — and be swept away," he said sharply when Pierson took too long to answer his question.

Pierson hesitated a moment longer, during which time he chewed on the corner of his lip while his eyes lost focus, as though he was trying to decide how to answer the question. Finally, he said, "Jenny. We were arguing about Jenny. We've argued about a lot of things over the years, but just recently Jenny and the hotel have been what we've argued about the most."

Nathan said nothing as the older man fell silent, giving him time to think, knowing that most people cannot stand silence without good cause and will seek to fill it. Soon enough Pierson did just that.

"I want Jenny to stick around and help run the hotel. I want her to go to the local university to study business and finance, maybe accounting, if she must go," he said in a voice that dared the two police officers to suggest that he was being unreasonable, which was clearly the reaction he was used to getting from his wife. "Tracey, though, she thinks we should let Jenny go wherever she wants, and study whatever she wants. She won't get a student loan to pay for her studies because our income from this place is just over some figure the government set, though, so if she goes to university, I'll have to pay for it. Surely if my money is paying for her to go, I should have some say in what she studies." He shook his head, as though he had difficulty understanding his wife's thinking, even though she wasn't there to put forward her argument. "Why should I pay for Jenny to go all the way across the country to study, when there's a perfectly good university just down the road. And why should I pay for her to study stuff she'll never make any money from, when she could be learning how to help with the family business.

"It's not like she wants to be a doctor or something. I could deal with that, if that's what she wanted."

"So, you argued with your wife about your daughter, an argument that caused you to hit her," Nathan said. "What happened after that?"

"I apologised," Pierson said. "At least I tried to. Tracey wouldn't have it. She started coming out with all kinds of crap. It felt like she was trying to make me hit her again. The number of times she's done that. You'd think if she wanted to leave me, she'd do it. Hell, at times like that I wish she would. If I wasn't sure I'd lose the hotel, I'd leave her. I bit my tongue and left, went back through to the hotel and hid away in the office while I took care of some paperwork."

"What did your wife do after the argument?"

Pierson shrugged. "No idea, I didn't see her again, that was..." His voice faltered as the memory crashed in on him. "That was the last time I saw her, last time I spoke to her. We argued, I hit her, and I never saw her again." He sobbed the words, crying as only a man who has finally realised what he has lost could.

Unlike the uniformed officer at his side, who was looking at Pierson with barely concealed disgust, Nathan had experience of dealing with someone who had suffered as David Pierson was. It wasn't all that long ago that he had suffered his own tragic loss. He took Pierson's arm and led him down the passage and into the kitchen, where he sat him down at the table and set about making him a cup of tea.

When he found a bottle of whiskey in one of the cupboards, he added a generous slug to the mug to help Pierson deal with the shock and grief.

"You said you didn't see your wife again following your argument," Nathan said once Pierson had finished his laced tea and his grief had, for the time being, run its course. "Did you hear her when she came home and returned her jacket to the hall closet?"

Pierson shook his head. "I'm a very deep sleeper. Once my head hits the pillow, I'm out for the count until my alarm goes off in the morning. Tracey and Jenny have both said that a bomb could go off under me and I wouldn't know about it, but the moment my alarm goes off I'm awake." His voice remained tremulous with grief, nonetheless he was more in control of it than he had been before being led into the kitchen.

"That would explain why you didn't respond when I was ringing the bell to be let in after getting locked out," Nathan remarked in a voice that was studiously non-accusatory. "Your wife must have made it home shortly after I returned to the hotel, assuming nothing delayed her along the way, which means your daughter would most likely have still been awake. Is it possible that she could have argued with her mother?" He knew he was courting an angry and potentially violent outburst with his question, but it was something he had to ask, no matter how much he might prefer not to, if he was going to get to the bottom of the murder of Tracey Pierson.

Pierson's eyes flashed angrily, and the skin of his face and neck flushed crimson, but the alcohol in his tea appeared to have had the effect of robbing him of the ability to react as he would have liked. When he found himself unable to verbalise an appropriate response, let alone produce one physically, he sighed heavily and reluctantly answered the question that had been put to him.

"They might have," he admitted. "They're both pretty peaceful people, but when their backs are up they can be harsh, and their tongues get pretty sharp. If they did argue about something, I wouldn't have heard it, but if you're trying to suggest that Jenny killed her mother, you're dead wrong." His eyes flashed again, but as before his anger faded as quickly as it had flared, thanks to the mellowing effect of the whiskey. "Jenny'll shout and swear when she's angry, but she hasn't got a violent bone in her body. Thank god she didn't inherit that from me."

"That may be so, Mr Pierson, but you can never be sure what a person will do when they're really angry about something," Nathan remarked. "Do you own a meat tenderiser?" he asked, looking around the cosy kitchen for any sign of where such an implement might usually reside. He couldn't see anywhere obvious, but that didn't really surprise him, a tenderiser wasn't something that most people kept on display.

For a moment Pierson looked as though he was going to launch into a defence of his daughter, but then he seemed to realise that words were not going to help. With an effort that seemed to suggest the move required more energy than he had just then, he pushed himself to his feet and took two steps across the kitchen to a pair of drawers under the counter by the sink.

He pulled open the first drawer and looked through it, closing it when he failed to find what he was looking for. The search of the second drawer took longer, and quickly assumed a panicked intensity as Pierson pulled it out as far as it would go so he could rummage through it desperately.

After nearly a minute of failure he began pulling out the contents and scattering them across the counter, so he could better see everything. It seemed like a desperate effort to find something that was clearly missing, but after two minutes he uttered a cry of triumph and turned away from the drawer, his hand held high. Clutched in his fist was a meat tenderiser.

"I told you Jenny didn't do it," Pierson said.

"I never said she did," Nathan said, his tone bland and uninflected as he sought to avoid saying or doing anything that might provoke the new-made widower's anger. He didn't want to do that unless it was absolutely necessary. He took the utensil from Pierson, so he could examine it; the chances were slim to the point of barely being worth considering, but he knew he couldn't discount the possibility that a new tenderiser had been bought to replace the murder weapon planted in his room, at least not without checking it out.

He needed only the briefest of examinations to satisfy himself that what he held was no replacement for the item used to kill Tracey Pierson. The tenderiser in his hand was clean, but it lacked the shine of something brand new, and along the handle was a worn and peeling manufacturer's label; only age could have made the label look the way it did, and it left Nathan with no doubts that the tenderiser had been hidden away in the back of the drawer for some time.

"However, I am going to need to take her fingerprints and yours." Nathan quickly held up a hand to forestall the protest he could see forming on Pierson's lips. "It's a formality, nothing more," he said. "In order to eliminate you both, officially, from my inquiry, I need to check your fingerprints against those on the murder weapon. If it makes you feel any better, even Constable Havers and I will be having our fingerprints checked."

16

"Why did you say we are being fingerprinted along with David and Jennifer Pierson?" Havers asked of Nathan when they returned to the office.

"Because we are," Nathan said. He could see the annoyance Havers was trying to conceal and it made him realise how inexperienced his reluctant partner was. He wished he had Stephen Burke to help him with the investigation, or even Detective Constable Georgius, who was his partner of recent times.

"But why? Surely you don't think I'm the murderer, and since you're now in charge of the investigation, you can't be a suspect."

Nathan smiled briefly. "Two reasons. Firstly, it's a means of reassuring the Piersons that it's only procedure and intended to help establish that they aren't responsible for the murder; if they know we are being fingerprinted as well, they are less likely to refuse to cooperate or make life difficult. Secondly, we need to prove conclusively that I didn't touch the murder weapon — we're going to have enough problems with that, given that I am currently in charge of the case — and since you neglected to wear gloves, we also need to eliminate your fingerprints from those found on the murder weapon.

"It's not going to be easy to do at the moment because our ability to communicate with the outside world is limited, so we'll have to do everything the old-fashioned way, and then have it all double-checked once communications are back up and running."

"Even if you are able to prove that you never touched the tenderiser, and neither did David or Jennifer Pierson, and you manage to eliminate my fingerprints," Havers looked suitably abashed at the mistake he had made, which he hoped wouldn't compromise the limited evidence they had, "we still won't be any closer to solving Tracey's murder."

"We will have reduced the suspect list by three, though, and that's good," Nathan said. Since the suspect list currently stood at over twenty, including all the guests and staff at the hotel, and should probably include at least some of the village's residents as well, removing three names from it was a step in the right direction. "Not only that but we'll have confirmed some more of Tracey Pierson's final movements. The jacket proves that she came home after I saw her, as she said she was going to do, and, if we can establish that the fingerprints on the tenderiser used to kill Tracey Pierson don't belong to any of the Piersons, we'll be able to say with some confidence that she went out again. We just have to find out where she went and who she went to see."

"Do you think it could be her lover?" Havers asked. After making the mistake of handling the murder weapon while not wearing gloves, he was keen to do or say something that would make it clear to the inspector that he wasn't a complete idiot. "Could he have killed her?"

Nathan considered that for a short while as he leant back in his commandeered swivel chair in his commandeered office. "It's possible," he said finally, leaning forward again. "It's certainly something we need to check out, which makes identifying him a matter of importance. Mrs Pierson's phone was taken to town, along with her body, and we won't know what, if anything, the forensic specialists have found on it until the storm passes and we can make a phone call without missing half of what is said, when we can get through at all, or we can get an email. We might be able to get somewhere with her computer, but only if it isn't password-protected; I'm not going to hold my breath on that.

"To be honest, I don't think whoever she was having an affair with had anything to do with her death, not unless something changed significantly in the time it took for her to get home. He was already out there in the woods with her; I can't think of a reason why, if he was of a mind to kill her, he would wait until she got home to kill her and then carry her body back out to the woods. Not only would that have increased his chances of getting caught, it would have put him to a lot of unnecessary effort."

"Maybe you being there forced him to change his plans," Havers said. "You said you disturbed Tracey and her lover, and that when you made it round the bend in the path all you could see of the guy was his back. Maybe he met Tracey out there with the intention of killing her, but when he realised there was a possible witness he decided to be cautious and kill her later."

"Maybe," Nathan agreed doubtfully. "But based on what I overheard of their conversation, I think it more likely that he would have killed David Pierson, if he was going to kill anyone. He got quite worked up over the abuse that Tracey suffered at David's hands. Regardless of whether I believe that Tracey's lover killed her, we need to find out who he is and speak to him. At the least we'll be able to eliminate him from our list of suspects, which will get us a little closer to finding our killer, and if we're lucky he'll know something that will lead us to the person we're after."

"And you think we'll find Tracey's lover by going through her things?" Havers wasn't sure about that. He wasn't an expert on extra-marital affairs, he had been happily married for over twenty years, but it seemed to him that if Tracey Pierson had kept anything that could identify her lover amongst her possessions, her husband would almost certainly have found it long ago.

"It's our best shot right now," Nathan said, though he had his own doubts. "Before we start that search, however, I need you to brave the elements, if you're willing, and go to the station." It was only about a quarter of a mile away, but with gale-force winds and lashing rain, not to mention lightning that split the darkness three times a minute, going to the station, let alone getting back again, was dangerous. "I'll understand if you're not prepared to make the trip, but we need the fingerprint kit, evidence bags in case we find anything, the murder weapon so we can make the fingerprint comparisons, and latex gloves to be sure we don't ruin any evidence we might find."

Havers had been uncertain about taking the risk of going out into the fury of the storm but the last item on the list of things Nathan wanted made up his mind to do it. He had already potentially ruined whatever fingerprints were on the tenderiser through his incompetence, he didn't want to put any more evidence at risk.

If he had to choose between the fury of his superiors if his mistakes allowed a murderer to walk free and the fury of the storm, he knew which he preferred.

17

While Havers put his life into God's hands, Nathan went looking for Louisa. It wasn't just a desire to see how she was coping with the weather-enforced restriction, he needed her help, if she was willing to provide it.

He found her in the bar, along with two-thirds of the hotel's guests, who were dealing with the situation in the most appropriate way available to them, by wetting their insides, something he wished he could join them in.

"Sorry to interrupt, got a minute, Lou?" he asked, intruding as politely as he could on the conversation his friend was having with her companions.

"Sure. Excuse me," Louisa said to her fellow holidaymakers as she pushed her chair back and got to her feet. "What's up?" she asked of her friend.

Nathan didn't answer straightaway, instead he led her away from the table, and away from the others in the bar. He didn't stop until he found a quiet corner where they couldn't be overheard. With every guest but for himself and Louisa as suspects in his murder case, he didn't want to take a chance on one of them overhearing something that, when gossiped around, would help the killer.

"Have you had any luck connecting to the internet?" Nathan asked. "I mean since I checked my email on your computer."

"No. I was getting an intermittent connection for a while, just enough to be annoying, without being good enough to do anything," Louisa told him. She preferred no signal to one that claimed to be there but couldn't be connected to, that was a tease that made her want to grind her teeth in frustration and swear. "That stopped a while back, though. I can't even get a suggestion of a signal now, either through the hotel's wi-fi or my phone. Why?"

Nathan would have grimaced in annoyance, but he had expected the answer, so he was prepared for it. "I was hoping you'd be able to email Stephen a list of names to check out for me, see if there's anything in the background of any of the guests that would give them a motive for murder. I want to know what he can find out about the Pierson family as well, see if they've got any enemies or a history of trouble. Something, anything, that would explain why someone decided to kill Tracey Pierson and dump her body in the woods." He sighed and fell silent for a moment. "If you can't get through, though, you can't. I'll just have to wait until the storm dies down and hope I have better luck elsewhere."

"I can send the email for you," Louisa said. She smiled at the look of confusion on Nathan's face. As always, it amused her that someone who wasn't much older than her, someone who needed computers on a daily basis for his job, could be so clueless as to how they worked. "I can't guarantee when it will go through, that'll depend on when the computer manages to get a connection."

"If you can't get a connection, how can you send the email?" Nathan had long since given up being embarrassed by his lack of knowledge when it came to computers and modern technology. He wasn't quite a luddite, but he did feel like a bit of a throwback when it came to all things modern; no matter how much he might need computers and their associated systems, he couldn't seem to come to grips with them, at least not with the ease and proficiency that others did.

Louisa used computers all the time, even more so now that she had her own website and was building herself an online news empire, and Stephen Burke was a dedicated gaming enthusiast who spent as much on a top-quality computer system as many people did on a good quality second-hand car.

"Easy. I can write the email and send it, and as long as the laptop's on, it will keep trying to send the message until it does so successfully. I don't even need to be anywhere near it, it'll do it automatically. It's kind of like an automatic redial thing," Louisa explained, sure that Nathan would at least understand that.

"Oh, okay." Nathan half understood what Louisa meant, and since he didn't want her to try any further to explain it to him, he nodded as if he knew just what she was talking about. "Let's go get this email written then. If you're willing, I could do with your help on something else afterwards."

Louisa didn't hesitate. She knew Nathan well enough to know that he wouldn't ask her for help if he didn't really need it. "Sure, you know me, always happy to help out. Besides, it's not like there's much else I can do." She looked out the window in disgust at the display of power nature was putting on as she said that. "Floyd Mantle isn't going to be around to help me with the article about the ocelots anytime soon, so I'm at a loose end; I've been talking to people, getting their stories, but, so far, no-one has a story that's good enough to keep me from helping you out."

It didn't surprise Nathan that Louisa was trying to use her time productively by coming up with stories for her website. He could only imagine how she must be fretting about what was happening with the site while it sat in the dubious hands of her recently employed and inexperienced assistant.

"Have you considered writing a story about the storm?" he asked. He was pleased to see that he had confused his friend, it made up for her confusing him by talking about computers when she knew he didn't understand them.

"What do you mean?" Louisa asked. Her mind raced as she tried to figure out what he could be on about before he could explain it to her, she didn't get there.

"Why not write a story about how a sudden, serious storm has a major effect on such a small community," Nathan suggested. "Not only can you get the stories of everyone stuck here, but you can add your own insight and experiences, plus you've got the addition of how everyone is reacting to the possibility of being stuck here with a murderer, while a murder investigation goes on."

"I could interview the other guests and the staff and get stories from all sides." Louisa quickly warmed to the idea. "You're a genius."

18

Jennifer Pierson pushed open the door that led from the hotel into the connecting house she shared with her parents, parent now, and preceded the group with her over the threshold.

"Dad," she called out, standing in the passage with one hand on the door, waiting to close it once everyone was through. "Dad, where are you?" The lack of a response worried her and turning to her guests, she said, "The living room's through there," she indicated a doorway a few steps away, "would you mind waiting in there while I see if I can find dad?"

"Of course, no problem," Nathan said agreeably, before leading Louisa and Constable Havers into the room they had been directed to.

Nathan took a seat on the sofa without hesitation, as did Louisa, but Havers hovered uncomfortably near the window, where he wouldn't feel in the way. Nathan knew the constable wasn't happy that he had brought along Louisa, a civilian, for assistance, but the way he saw it, there wasn't much choice; they needed someone who knew computers better than either of them, and the only person who was available and not on the list of suspects was Louisa.

"Do you think Mr Pierson's alright?" Havers asked when the silence in the room had stretched on for almost a minute.

Nathan gave an uncertain shrug. "Under the circumstances, I think it unlikely that Mr Pierson is alright, but to what degree he isn't remains to be seen."

“Could he have done something stupid?”

Havers’ tone made it clear what he meant by something stupid and, as he did whenever he heard the phrase, Nathan wondered why people thought it okay to label an act that stemmed from despair and emotional trauma in such a negative way. It was only through the support of friends and family that he had not done something that people might label stupid — he had had thoughts of it — when he lost his wife and kids.

“If you mean, could Mr Pierson be feeling so low after the murder of his wife that he has decided he can’t go on, that’s possible,” Nathan said. “Though I can’t say that I thought it a possibility when we left him earlier. He was depressed, certainly, but he seemed to be coping about as well as a man can be expected to under the circumstances.” As he spoke, he wondered if he had done the right thing when he left David Pierson, if he shouldn’t have left Havers to keep an eye on the bereaved husband. “If he’s not home, I imagine he’s keeping himself busy somewhere in the hotel.”

He knew from his own experience that although grief robbed a person of energy and enthusiasm, making it hard to do anything, keeping busy was one of the best ways to get through it. Keeping active and keeping the mind distracted was the best way to fight the urge to do something that couldn’t be undone.

The trio were in the living room for a little over five minutes before Jennifer Pierson appeared, alone. The absence of her father made them all worry, until she spoke.

“Dad was sleeping. I think he had a few whiskeys, there’s a bottle on the bedside table, and crashed out,” Jennifer told them. “He’ll be down once he’s dressed.”

There was nothing for them to do then but wait some more and do their best to ignore the noise as the wind and rain hammered at the window.

“Hi,” David Pierson croaked from the living room doorway.

"Hello, Mr Pierson. I'm sorry to have disturbed you while you were resting," Nathan said, getting to his feet. "I hope you don't mind, but we brought along someone to assist us with our search of the house, specifically the computer your wife used." He indicated Louisa, who had risen to her feet at his side. "This is Louisa Orchard, she isn't a police officer, but she does know more about computers than either me or Constable Havers. If you would prefer us not to make use of a civilian in these extraordinary circumstances, I'll understand, and we'll muddle through as best we can."

Pierson's response was a barely perceptible shrug and a mumbled, "Don't care."

"Okay, since that's settled, I think we should get started. And before we do anything else we should get the fingerprints out of the way. It would be best, I think," Nathan said, "if we do this in the kitchen, since we've got to do it the old-fashioned way, with ink, and that can get a little messy."

It had been a long time since Nathan had to use ink and card to take someone's fingerprints, and even Havers, who wasn't lucky enough to have a fingerprinting machine at his station, was out of practice. The result was that it took longer than anticipated, with a few false starts along the way, before they succeeded in getting a complete set of prints from the four of them — it wasn't necessary for them to take Louisa's fingerprints since she wasn't a suspect and hadn't touched anything that needed checking.

Despite the problems, it took less time to get the fingerprints done than it did for them to get the ink cleaned off their fingers.

Once the fingerprints were done, it was time to start the search of the house for anything that might lead them to either Tracey Pierson's lover or her murderer, assuming they weren't the same person. The search was kicked off in the master bedroom, where most of Tracey Pierson's things were, while Louisa did what she could with the computer in the utility room that had been made into a tiny office.

Neither David nor Jennifer Pierson stuck around to watch while the two police officers made their search. David Pierson, when asked if he wanted to stay and observe, admitted to having no interest in how the search was conducted, nor in what was found, he simply wanted his wife's killer caught, as quickly as possible. Jennifer in the meantime was more concerned with making sure that her father was alright; whatever grief she felt over the loss of her mother was being overshadowed by her concern for her father.

Nathan was glad not to have either of the bereaved breathing down his neck during the search. At the same time, he worried, probably unnecessarily, that if anything was found that incriminated either of the Piersons there might be an accusation of it being planted for them to deal with.

"I think I've got something, sir," Havers said, extracting a large, manila envelope from a drawer in the chest he was searching.

Nathan was happy to abandon the wardrobe he had been investigating in favour of finding out what it was Havers had discovered.

He had searched the drawers under the bed, a chest of drawers containing David Pierson's clothes, the vanity in the bay window, and the wardrobe; all without finding so much as a hint of a reason for Tracey Pierson's murder, let alone anything that might lead him to the person responsible. He hadn't even found anything to narrow down who it was that Tracey Pierson had been having an affair with, so he was glad of a distraction.

He hoped Havers had found something that was connected to their case; if he hadn't, Nathan worried that their search was going to prove to be a waste of time, though he realised there was still the rest of the house to go through.

"What've you got?" Nathan asked of the constable as he crossed the room to join him.

"Not sure, sir, but I found these hidden under Tracey's clothes," Havers said, holding up the pair of envelopes he had discovered. "This one's addressed to David Pierson, at the hotel."

"Curious," Nathan said absently, holding out a hand for the envelopes. There could easily be a simple reason why Tracey Pierson had hidden an envelope under her clothes, several reasons in fact, and none of them needed to have anything to do with it having her husband's name on it. Despite that he was sure that the envelope being meant for David Pierson had everything to do with it being hidden by Tracey.

Before he looked inside he examined the outside of the envelope, in case it could reveal anything about the sender.

"Neat handwriting," he observed, noting the precise way David Pierson's name, and the address of the hotel, had been printed on the envelope. There was nothing about the careful writing that was likely to give anything away about the hand responsible, though, at least not without proper forensic analysis. "Clearly whoever opened this doesn't share the same sense of neatness."

Havers wasn't sure if he was supposed to respond to that or not, but since the comment seemed directed at the envelope and the ragged tear where it had been ripped open, he kept quiet.

"Have you spoken to anyone in connection to the murder who comes from Portsmouth?" Nathan asked.

"No," Havers said. "Why?"

Nathan held up the envelope and tapped the stamp in the top right corner. "It's postmarked from Portsmouth, and was sent last month, so it would have arrived here no more than three weeks ago," he said, clarifying what he was indicating with his finger. "I wonder what's in it, and why it's been hidden away; let's have a look, shall we."

Without waiting for Havers to respond, Nathan pulled open the envelope, so he could dump the contents out on the chest of drawers.

What appeared was sufficiently surprising to render both the inspector and the constable speechless for almost a minute.

"I think it's safe to say that someone knew about Tracey Pierson's affair," Nathan said when he recovered his voice.

With as much professional detachment as he could manage, he flipped through the half dozen sheets of A4 paper the envelope had held; each sheet of paper was a computer printout made up of six photographs, for a total of thirty-six racy pictures showing a couple in the throes of passion.

The couple were clearly a man and a woman, and it was just as clear that they were very much into the acts they had been pictured performing. The couple were so into them that it was obvious neither was aware that someone with a camera was spying on them.

"The woman is obviously Tracey Pierson," Nathan said. The printouts were not of the best quality: the size of the images made it hard to make out details and the paper had crinkled where it was too thin for the ink that had saturated it. Despite that, he could think of no-one else the woman could be. "I've no idea who the man is, though. How about you, any idea who he is?" he asked of Havers.

Havers picked up each printout in turn and scrutinised it carefully, wishing as he did that he had a magnifying glass. When he was done he shook his head.

"His face isn't visible in any of the pictures, as far as I can tell," Havers said. "Given the quality of them, I don't think I could put a name to the guy if it was me in them."

"I was afraid you were going to say that," Nathan said with an unhappy sigh. "I suspect there's only one person, aside from either of us, we can be sure isn't the man in the pictures, and that's David Pierson. Something else we can be sure of, David might not have known about his wife's affair — he clearly didn't receive the pictures or Tracey wouldn't have hidden them amongst her clothes — but someone, someone in Portsmouth, knew and wanted him to know. Why else send him the pictures." Nathan's brow furrowed as something occurred to him. "I don't get why she kept them." His voice betrayed the depths of his confusion. "I get why she would have wanted to keep them where David couldn't find them, but why keep them at all, that's tempting fate."

"Maybe she got a kick out of them," Havers suggested.

"Perhaps, but I'd have expected her to be more concerned that someone was trying to reveal her affair than titillated." Nathan sighed. "I guess this at least gives us something of a motive for her murder; someone was either unhappy about the affair, maybe the wife or girlfriend of Tracey's lover, and they were hoping that David would do something about it, or they were trying to blackmail Tracey and it went wrong."

"Maybe David did do something about it," Havers said. "Maybe he's lying about not knowing about the affair, and he's been faking all the grief."

"That's definitely something we have to consider," Nathan said. "The only thing we know right now, though, is that the person who sent the pictures is either from Portsmouth or they had a reason to be there in the last six weeks. When we've finished searching the house, I want you to question all the guests and staff about where they live and any trips they may have taken recently. In the meantime..." Nathan picked up the second envelope and emptied out the contents so he could find out what else Tracey Pierson had kept hidden from her husband.

19

Nathan stood in the doorway for a few moments and looked from Jennifer Pierson, who was curled up on the sofa, her feet tucked under her, to her father, who stared into space from the armchair he occupied.

"Have you found anything?" Jennifer asked when she realised the inspector was there.

Nathan nodded slowly as he left the doorway and entered the room. "We found a couple of envelopes hidden amongst your mother's clothes. I'm sorry to say this, but their contents confirm that she was having an affair. I realise this isn't going to be easy for you, either of you, but I am going to need you both to take a look at what we've found, if you wouldn't mind putting these on." He held out a pair of latex gloves to the Piersons.

"Why do we need them?" Jennifer asked as she pulled on the gloves.

"So you don't smudge or ruin any fingerprints or DNA there is on the evidence." Nathan didn't say so, but it was also so that if the fingerprints of either Jennifer or David Pierson were to be found on any of the contents or either of the envelopes, they could be certain it meant they had handled them previously. That would suggest, almost certainly prove in fact, that they did know about the affair, despite their assertions to the contrary. "Have you seen this envelope before, Mr Pierson?" Nathan asked, holding out the envelope addressed to him. "It was found under some clothes in the chest of drawers belonging to your wife."

David Pierson took the envelope, so he could examine it, but quickly shook his head. "I don't recognise it," he said. "I get a fair number of envelopes at the hotel every month, all shapes and sizes and colours, but I'm sure I'd remember if I'd seen that one, I don't get many with handwritten addresses."

Nathan wasn't sure how big a pinch of salt to take that statement with, but since he couldn't prove otherwise at that time — it was always possible that Pierson was telling the truth — he accepted it at face value.

"Do you know, or did your wife know, anyone who lives in Portsmouth?" he asked.

The question required a few moments of thought. "I don't," Pierson said finally. "I imagine we've had a few people from there stay at the hotel over the years, we've had guests from all over the country, and from other countries as well, but I couldn't give you any names for guests who came from Portsmouth.

"I couldn't say if Tracey does...did. She never mentioned anyone, but she wasn't all that close with her family, and she used to say that no matter what job she had she always kept too busy for friends. Why do you ask?"

"That's where the envelope was sent from," Nathan said. "How about your suppliers, or the organisations you deal with — I imagine you belong to several organisations as part of your business — are any of them based in Portsmouth or have connections with there?"

Pierson shrugged. "Sorry, but I've no idea without checking. None of the organisations have held any meetings or conferences in Portsmouth. I'm sure I'd remember if they had, but beyond that..." He shrugged again. "A lot of the companies and organisations are based in one place but have offices and depots and who knows what all over the place. I can take a look if you want, see if I've dealt with any offices or departments in Portsmouth. It'll take me a while, though," he warned. "Tracey used to deal with the accounts more than me, she was better at that stuff; I deal with the day to day stuff at the hotel."

Nathan wasn't too sure how true that was. In the time that he had been at the hotel prior to Tracey Pierson's murder, he had seen far more of her than he had of her husband. He stored it away in the back of his mind in case it should prove important and turned to Jennifer Pierson. "Do you know anyone who lives in Portsmouth?"

Jennifer shook her head without hesitation.

"Well, regardless of whether either of you know someone in Portsmouth, it's clear that someone in Portsmouth knew your wife, well enough to know that she was having an affair," Nathan said. Taking the envelope back he removed the contents, so he could pass them to David Pierson. "And they wanted to make sure you knew about the affair as well. The pictures are not the best quality, but there is at least one that shows your wife's face clearly. The face of the man is not visible, at least not in these pictures; it's possible, however, that you can make out some identifying feature.

"I appreciate that they are not what you want to be looking at right now," he said compassionately, noting the tension in David Pierson and the way his hands shook and threatened to either screw up the images or tear them apart. "Believe me, I do understand what you're thinking and feeling, but if you can identify the man with your wife, I need to know. I need to speak to him and find out what, if anything, he knows about your wife's death."

"You...you think he killed her?" Pierson asked as he fought the urge to destroy the images in his hands.

"My initial feeling, and I admit I could be wrong, is no," Nathan said with as much conviction as he could project. "Although we don't currently know who your wife's lover is, we do know enough to be able to say it's unlikely that he killed her. He might, however, know who would have been interested enough in the affair to try and reveal it. It's important that we find out who sent those pictures because, and I stress this is just my opinion, it seems likely that if someone wanted to expose your wife's affair they wanted to stop it, which means they might have been willing to go so far as to commit murder to do so."

Pierson closed his eyes, as if by doing so he could block out the inspector's words.

"So, you think the person who sent those pictures," Jennifer gestured to the sheets of paper suffering at her father's hands, "killed mum?"

Nathan shrugged. "It's a possibility we need to look into. I'm really sorry, Mr Pierson, but I need you to look at the pictures and tell me if you can see anything that will help us identify the man in them." Nathan's voice was as kindly and compassionate as he could make it.

20

Bone weary, and more than a little frustrated, Nathan perched himself on the low filing cabinet that sat behind the desk in the converted box room. There was only the one chair in the room and that was occupied by Louisa, who was at the computer, so he had no choice but to perch where he was if he wanted to be able to see what Louisa was doing and talk to her at the same time.

"I take it things are not going well," Louisa remarked over her shoulder as she continued with what she was doing on the computer.

Nathan responded to that with a shrug that Louisa couldn't see that could have meant anything. "Right now I have to consider everyone who was staying at the hotel when Mrs Pierson was killed a suspect, which means I have more than twenty suspects. That's more than I like dealing with, especially since I'm having to do this all without being able to check backgrounds or fingerprints, let alone DNA." He sighed heavily.

Louisa chuckled.

"What's with the laughter?" Nathan asked, fixing the back of his friend's head with a fierce look.

"You, acting as though you're unhappy about having to handle this investigation with no modern tech support." Louisa laughed again. "You know as well as I do that you couldn't be happier. You've always trusted your instincts more than science and technology. You're in your element." She had spun the swivel chair away from the computer and now watched Nathan intently. "Come on, admit it, you wish all crimes were like this. If you had your way, you'd go back to the seventies or eighties, before technology and DNA took over."

"I'd rather there were fewer suspects," Nathan said. "Twenty plus complicates things a little too much, even if most of them are pretty obviously not involved."

"So, you've got no idea who's behind the murder?" Louisa was surprised, it wasn't like Nathan to be completely clueless when it came to a case.

Nathan shook his head. "I didn't say that. What I've found so far suggests the murder has something to do with the affair Tracey Pierson was having. Though whether she was killed by her husband or daughter because of the affair, her lover to conceal it, or by the person who was trying to expose it, remains to be determined. My money's on the person who tried to expose the affair by sending pictures of Tracey and her lover to David Pierson, but we don't currently have the first clue who that person is.

"I don't suppose you've found anything on there from a person in Portsmouth, have you?" Nathan asked, gesturing to the computer Louisa had been checking for him. He hoped she had found something, anything, to help him narrow down his list of suspects.

"No," Louisa said with a shake of her head. "But that doesn't mean much. I can only access what's on the hard drive, the offline email and internet data her system has stored, at the moment, which probably isn't even half of what you need." She saw the disappointment in Nathan's face and continued quickly. "The offline emails do show that Tracey Pierson was being harassed by someone, a female to judge by the tone and content of the emails, over her affair. I've found four of the emails sent by LaMeD1977@gmail.com so far, and they're all pretty similar in tone, *'leave my husband alone, you dirty whore', 'I know what you're doing, you bitch', 'stop or I'll make you sorry'.* I'm sure you don't need me to tell you the rest of it."

"No, I don't," Nathan agreed. It required only minimal imagination on his part to guess at what else was in the emails; he was sure they contained all the vitriol of a woman scorned, something which could easily lead to murder, and had on numerous occasions in the past. "Clearly Tracey Pierson wasn't the only married party involved in the affair." He shook his head, as if dismayed by such a failure of faithfulness. "Is there anything in the emails that might help us figure out who Tracey Pierson's lover or his wife are?"

"Nothing blatant, like a name and address," Louisa said. "That'd be too easy. But I'd say the wife being cheated on was born in seventy-seven — a lot of people put their birth year into their email addresses and screen names — which would put her a bit over forty. It's not the brightest thing a person can do, but people still do it. I'd also say the wife's name has the letters L-A-M-E-D in it. Most likely it's a combination of the first letters of her first and last name, and perhaps her middle initial."

"Come on, you can't possibly know that," Nathan said disbelievingly.

"Not for definite, no, but in my line of work it helps to know something about email addresses and usernames and the like, they can tell you a lot about a person, especially if they lack the sense to take even normal precautions. One of the first things I learnt on the cyber security course I took is that people have a habit of falling into patterns when it comes to creating usernames and passwords, and far too often they use names and birthdays, either their own or that of someone in their family," Louisa said. "The odds are better than even that the person threatening Tracey Pierson has a first name beginning L-A and a last name beginning with M-E-D. If that isn't it, the letters will come from her name in some fashion. Combine that with the year, seventy-seven, and the fact that they are most likely from Portsmouth, and you've taken your first steps to identifying the lover's wife.

"Have you got anyone who fits the bill on your list of suspects?"

"No-one I can think of off the top of my head," he admitted, which didn't mean much since they knew so little about the people on the suspects list." Havers is doing his best, though, to see if he can find someone with a connection to Portsmouth. I'll have him look for names and dates of birth that match as well. Have you got anything else that might help me?"

"Not at the moment. It's taken me this long just to dig out what I have," Louisa told him. "I think Mrs Pierson may have had a second email account and web browser, which she most likely used for contacting her lover. I've spotted a few hints buried away and tracking them down is next on my agenda. Hopefully I'll be able to find out something more useful from it."

"Fingers crossed. Do you think you can print off everything you've found so far, and whatever else you find?"

21

Accompanied by Jennifer Pierson, Nathan returned to the hotel from the house, relieved that he could do so without going outside.

The storm continued to rage, with no sign of abating, and he could only hope that no-one was unlucky enough to have been caught out in it. The local search and rescue team would be taking their lives into their hands if they got a call to find someone while the wind and rain continued with their current intensity, and that was without considering the danger that came from the lightning that flashed across the sky several times a minute.

The two of them may have been walking side by side, but they might as well have been at opposite ends of the country. Both were preoccupied with the murder of Tracey Pierson, though for different reasons.

Nathan was focused on trying to figure out who among the guests — now that he had reason to believe that the murderer was from Portsmouth, he felt confident that he could take the staff off his list of suspects, temporarily at least — had killed the adulterous Tracey Pierson. Jennifer on the other hand was struggling with the grief caused by her mother's murder and wondering to what extent the loss of her mother was going to change her life.

Jennifer felt guilty at such selfish thinking but couldn't stop herself trying to work out what areas of her life were going to change, and whether those changes would be for the better or the worse. So much was uncertain, but one thing she was sure of was that it was going to be even harder for her to go away to university now. Her father had been reluctant to let her go before, now he was going to be even more keen for her to stay close to home to help him run the hotel.

"...find out you had anything to do with Tracey's murder..."

The voice was low, barely audible, but the anger and menace in it cut through Jennifer's distracted thinking and brought her back to the here and now. The hand on her arm, which applied sudden pressure when she opened her mouth to speak, told her that Nathan had heard the voice as well and wanted to hear more. She could hardly blame him for that.

When she took a moment to think about what she had been about to do, she was glad that Nathan had stopped her. As much as she wanted to rush down the passage and around the corner, so she could confront her mother's killer — not that she knew that that was who she would find — she didn't fancy coming face to face with someone who clearly had no problem with violence.

"You'll what?" It was hard to identify the second speaker because they were talking in a low voice that was filled with as much anger and menace as the man's, but it was clearly a female. *"You haven't got the guts to do anything. You've never had the guts. You should be thankful I went after her, not you, after your betrayal, but you know I could never hurt you, I love you, and once this bloody storm's out of the way you're going to come back with me and we're going to be a family again."*

Nathan listened to the woman in amazement. It was obvious that she was unstable, even from the small amount he had arrived in time to overhear; nobody stable would ever think they could get someone back by killing the person they were sleeping with, at least not permanently. They might get the object of their affections back for a while, but it would only be under threat of violence, and the moment that threat was gone, or the object of their desire saw an opportunity, they would be gone again.

While he continued to listen, Nathan debated what he should do: he could charge around the corner and arrest whoever he found there, or he could stay where he was and continue listening. It didn't take him long to decide which course of action was best. He hadn't yet heard anything that would stand up in court as proof that the woman was the murderer of Tracey Pierson, so arresting her would accomplish nothing other than to put her on her guard, which was the last thing he wanted to do.

With his hand still on Jennifer's arm to make sure she kept quiet, Nathan listened intently to the couple who continued to argue. He hoped that something would be said or done that would enable him to make an arrest and close the case, so he could return to his holiday.

"We'll never be a family again, Laura," the man said sharply. *"Never. We weren't even a family in the first place, it was just you, me, and the dog, and I preferred living with the dog. Living with you was a nightmare. I wish I'd never met you. Why do you think I left?"*

"Because of that whore. She enticed you away from me. I saw the pictures she sent you, they were enough to turn any man's head, and you've always been weak."

"I left you long before she sent me them, long before."

"You need looking after," Laura continued, as if she hadn't heard him. *"You need me to look after you. Come home and everything will be like it was before. It'll be perfect."*

"It was never perfect, except maybe right at the beginning," the man snapped, though his voice remained low, betraying his eagerness not to be overheard. *"That's the problem, Laura, and you're too crazy to see it, you think things are perfect when they're anything but, and your idea of perfect is enough to drive anyone away."*

"I'll change. I promise I'll change, just come back home with me," Laura pleaded, her voice betraying how close to tears she was.

"Whatever you want, I'll do it. Anything. All you've got to do is come home. I'll be the perfect wife, John, you'll see."

"No." The man's voice was as hard as iron. *"I'll never go back with you, not to that house, not anywhere. You need help. I wish you could see that."*

As quick as that the pleading note vanished from the woman's voice to be replaced by venom as deadly as that in any cobra's bite. *"You think you'll find yourself another little whore to play at being in love with? Maybe one that doesn't have a husband and kid this time. You're mine, John, mine. I don't care how many times you try and leave me, I'll find you, just like I did this time, and I'll kill whatever whore you're with. And next time I won't be half as gentle as I was with that Pierson bitch, I'll make her suffer, and I might even make you watch."*

Nathan had heard enough, enough to let him make an arrest and enough to let him hold whoever he arrested in custody while he worked on finding solid evidence. It would have made little difference if he hadn't for his hand was forced by a loud, shocked gasp from Jennifer. He could hardly blame her for her reaction, but he would have preferred it if she had managed to keep from voicing her shock so audibly.

Any surprise he might have hoped for went with the gasp, and before he could hurry around the corner to make his arrest the situation worsened. The door behind him, the door leading to the Piersons' house, opened with a bang, making Nathan turn quickly to see what was going on.

"Sorry," Louisa apologised. "It got away from me."

Nathan closed his mouth with a snap on the angry comment that threatened to escape him. He turned his back on his friend and hurried to the corner, where he saw a door swinging shut further along the passage, while at the far end he caught a glimpse of a blue top disappearing around a corner.

Never had he wished so greatly for the ability to split himself in two, so he could investigate both locations. It would have been alright if he could have said with certainty which way the woman went, since that was who he wanted to arrest. He couldn't, though.

Reluctantly, and with his teeth grinding with frustration, Nathan put aside his desire to chase wildly after a person he wouldn't recognise if he tripped over them and headed back to Jennifer and Louisa.

"Are they gone?" Jennifer asked needlessly.

Nathan nodded unhappily. "I'm not even sure who went which way, and on my own I'd be wasting my time chasing around for someone I didn't see and can't identify." It was frustrating to think that he had been so close to catching the killer, only for fate, in the form of his noisy friend and a gasp from Jennifer, to get in the way. "I don't suppose by some miracle you recognised either of the voices, did you?"

Jennifer shook her head sadly. She was just as unhappy about the killer's escape as Nathan, though there was a part of her, deep down, that was glad she didn't have to face her mother's murderer. She was afraid of what her reaction might have been, whether she would have broken down and collapsed in tears or launched herself at the woman, seeking revenge.

"What's going on?" Louisa wanted to know. She was sure that her noisy arrival had been less than timely, but she didn't know just how much so.

"I was about to make an arrest," Nathan informed his friend. He didn't want Louisa to feel too bad about her enabling the killer to get away, it was an accident after all, but he couldn't quash his annoyance completely. "Your unfortunately timed disturbance," he scowled, "provided her with just enough time to get away. I wasn't even able to get a glimpse of her, so I don't know who it is I should be arresting."

"Sorry, Nate," Louisa said contritely. She felt even worse about the door slipping out of her hand than she had before. "And I wasn't even coming through here for a good reason. I was only after some paper for the printer, there isn't much in the office. I looked around but couldn't find any and I thought it best to get some before I start printing what I've found for you and run out."

Nathan's scowl deepened. "Paper," he said disgustedly. He had had cases messed up by a number of things in the past, many of them silly and annoying, but never before by a need for printer paper.

"Sorry," Louisa apologised for a second time.

22

Nathan sat at a table in the most sheltered corner of the dining room, the printouts from Tracey Pierson's computer spread out in front of him. He read through them while eating, without really paying attention to the food he had ordered for his dinner. Mechanically, he dipped his fork to the plate, lifted it to his mouth, chewed, swallowed, and then repeated the process, all without looking down at his plate.

His attention was focused on the mass of paper as he searched for something, anything, that would help him to identify the person he had come so close to arresting. He was so intent on the printed emails, bills, and social media messages, that he didn't notice when he was joined at the table by Constable Havers. He was even oblivious to the display of power being put on by nature outside the window next to him, and to the noise being made inside as the guests sought to drown out the storm.

Only when he had put down the last sheet of paper did Nathan become aware of his surroundings. He didn't acknowledge Havers, though, or do any more than glance around the restaurant at his fellow diners, a few of whom were watching him, their eyes skipping from him to the papers on the table and back again. The rest seemed to be paying him no mind, though he was sure they were just as aware that he was now in charge of the murder investigation and just as interested in how it was going.

Lasagne, that was what he was eating, Nathan realised now that his attention was no longer consumed by the printouts. He had managed to get through fully two-thirds of it without being aware of what he had ordered. Now that he was he slowed down, so he could enjoy his food, which wasn't difficult since it was delicious.

Once his plate was clean and he had finished off his glass of coke — he had been tempted to order a cider but had decided against it since he had been co-opted into running an investigation — Nathan paid attention to Havers. As he did he wondered where Louisa was, he had expected her to join him for dinner, though it had taken him until then to notice that she hadn't. He didn't imagine that anything had happened to her, but it was unlike Louisa to miss out on a meal when he was paying.

"Did you find anything?" Nathan asked of Havers. He kept his voice low to be sure it wouldn't carry to the next table, which was closer than he liked just then. It would have been better, he realised, if he had waited until they were in private to ask the question, but he was feeling full after his meal and didn't want to move, unless he had to.

Havers shook his head. "I found two guests and one member of staff who were born in nineteen-seventy-seven," he said. "The two guests are male and female, and not travelling together, and the member of staff is female, she's the head of housekeeping. You said the person we're looking for is female, so I ignored the bloke. Of the women, neither is called Laura, and neither of them have a last name that begins either M-E-D or D. The housekeeper's name is Felicity Wood, and the guest is Susan McKinney." He paused to wet his throat with a sip from his own glass of coke. "I've checked out all the guests and staff, as much as I've been able..."

A tinkling sound, which could only have been made by breaking glass, cut across the conversations that filled the restaurant, silencing them. If that wasn't enough to make people stop talking and look around, what followed was.

"You clumsy bitch, look at the mess you've made."

Nathan didn't need to look to know that it was the large Mr Moore, he had learnt his name from the investigation's file, who had spoken. Most of the people in the dining room, after the briefest of glances, looked away in embarrassment. It came as no surprise to Nathan that the few people who showed unashamed interest in what was happening at the table occupied by the Moores were the same ones who had watched him as he read through his paperwork.

"What's the matter with you? Can't you even pick up a glass of wine without spilling it?" Moore demanded of his wife. "Look at you, look at your dress. That was brand new when you put it on. Do you have any idea how much it cost?"

It wasn't just natural and professional curiosity that made Nathan pay attention to what was going on, it was concern for the wife. He didn't think it likely that Moore would hit his wife, no matter how angry he was, not when there were so many witnesses around, including a uniformed constable, but it was always a possibility.

He was tempted to go over to remind Moore that he was there, simply to ensure that no violence occurred, but he realised that there was every chance he would only make things worse if he did so, something he was reluctant to do.

Mrs Moore mumbled something while dabbing at the wine she had spilt. The back of her neck had gone an unhealthy shade of red as she hunched her shoulders and gave every indication of wanting to isolate herself, as much as possible, from the people who were witness to her humiliation.

"You're damned right it cost a fortune," Moore said, speaking over the small amount of conversation that had started up again. "And if you think I'm just going to buy you another, you can think again. I'm probably going to have to pay for the carpet you've just ruined."

Nathan couldn't work out if Moore was speaking so loudly because it was natural for him to do so, or if he was doing so deliberately to embarrass his wife for her mistake and to make it clear that he spent a considerable amount of money on her. One thing that was certain to Nathan was that many of the people in the restaurant were being made to feel uncomfortable by the situation, himself included.

He had just concluded that he would have to do or say something when the matter was resolved, if perhaps not in the best way.

"Go on, get out of my sight," Moore snapped. "Get yourself cleaned up."

Helen Moore almost knocked over her chair in her haste to get out of her husband's sight. She looked neither left nor right as she hurried from the dining room, with the result that she bumped into several occupied chairs before she reached the doors, but she never once stopped to apologise. She didn't want to give anyone a chance to acknowledge what her husband had just put her through.

"I appreciate that this is a trying time, Mr Moore," Nathan said, taking the seat vacated by the man's embarrassed wife. "It's a trying time for all of us, being stuck here in the hotel by this storm, with a murder investigation being conducted. And that in trying times, little things can assume an out of context importance and cause us to act uncharacteristically."

Moore looked angrily across the table at the man who had sat himself down uninvited. "What're you on about?"

"I mean you should be careful not to take out your frustration with the situation on your wife," Nathan told him. "It's not fair on her, and it's not fair on everyone else here. We're all trying to have a nice meal and get through this storm as best we can."

"Get lost. Who the hell are you to tell me what I can do?" Moore demanded. "I'll do and say what I like, especially when it comes to my wife. If she doesn't like what I say to her, she shouldn't do stupid shit like spill wine. And if the rest of you don't like it..." He glared around the dining room, sharing what was clearly meant to be a look of intimidation with any who dared to so much as glance his way. "You can all go to hell. I didn't get where I am today by letting people tell me what I can and can't do."

Nathan's hand was closing around the warrant card in his pocket, which he hoped would convince the man across from him to cease with his belligerent attitude, when a scream, closely followed by a cry of pain and then a heavy thud, made everyone in the restaurant look up in surprise and alarm.

He was on his feet in an instant, and across the dining room and out the door in barely a quarter of a minute. He was moving so quickly that if someone had told him that he had run through the tables and diners to get to the door he wouldn't have been surprised.

Apart from registering that the scream had come from a woman, Nathan had no idea what had happened, or what he was going to find. He expected, however, to find something relatively simple, like a woman scared by a mouse or a spider or caught by surprise by a sudden flash of lightning that lent a terrifying aspect to a tree seen through a window. What he found when he reached the foyer was more serious.

Helen Moore was at the bottom of the stairs, not moving. She was on her back, her head near the front doors, which rattled and shook as they were assailed by the gale force winds outside, though she showed no sign of being aware of either the noise or the movement. One arm was trapped awkwardly under her, while the other was flung across the carpeted floor as though reaching for something or someone. Her left leg was straight and normal, but her right was bent back at an angle that anyone, even someone who lacked medical training, could have said was unnatural.

Unconscious or dead. Nathan couldn't say which was the case when he first entered the foyer, all he could be certain of was that she wasn't awake. He knew enough about injuries, of all sorts, to know that Helen Moore couldn't possibly be awake with the injuries she clearly had, not without screaming the place down.

The second thing Nathan noted, after taking in Helen Moore's position at the foot of the stairs and her injuries, was the figure kneeling over her. It wasn't that he had somehow missed the second person, it was just that his brain had prioritised the data it was receiving, and now that it had processed the most important elements of the situation it took in the secondary aspects, chief of which was the man.

"What happened?" Nathan asked as he strode across the small foyer, his fingers already reaching for Helen Moore's throat, so he could check for a pulse.

It took him several long moments to find what he was looking for, a slow steady beat that indicated Helen Moore was alive, and when he did he breathed a sigh of relief.

He had been so focused on his search for a pulse that he was oblivious to what was going on around him, but now noise washed over him. Shouts and cries, voices filled with pain and anger, protestations of innocence, questions, theories. Nathan became aware of all of it as he pushed himself to his feet and took in the chaos that filled the foyer.

Havers was on the floor, propped up against the counter, his eyes glazed, and a bloodstained handkerchief pressed to his mouth; Arthur Moore and Simon Bonner, the slim man who had been knelt over Helen Moore, were locked together in a combat that seemed to involve more grappling than actual trading of blows, though the occasional punch did land, and frequent, muffled insults.

One of the waiters from the dining room, along with Jennifer Pierson, was dancing around the grappling pair, trying to get close enough to separate them without getting injured in the process. Nathan surmised that that was what had happened to Havers — he had failed to avoid the flailing fists.

What the two men were fighting about, Nathan didn't have the first clue, though he supposed it might have something to do with Bonner having been found at the foot of the stairs with Moore's wife. It was not unusual, though often completely illogical, for the person or persons found with someone who had been injured to receive the blame for the injury, even if there was no blame to be assigned.

A wide area of clear space — as wide as the foyer would allow — had been left around the fighters, and another at the foot of the stairs, but the rest of the space was taken up by the guests from the dining room and the staff. As a group it seemed that they were uncertain which situation deserved their attention most: the fight or the unconscious Helen Moore.

It was much like traffic at the scene of a car crash, Nathan thought; no matter how nasty it was, or how disgusted they were by it, human nature wouldn't let them turn away and ignore it, they just had to look.

Nathan noted it all in an instant, though it was a few moments more before his brain processed it all. Once he had he sucked in a lungful of air and yelled, "Enough!" in a voice that could probably be heard throughout the hotel, and might even have been heard outside if not for the storm.

The shout was so sudden and so loud that it had the desired effect; Moore and Bonner broke off their fighting, so they could find out who had shouted and why. The pair of them looked as guilty as schoolboys caught doing something silly when they saw how many witnesses there was to their ineffectual fighting.

With a final shove, which sent Bonner to the floor, Moore hurried over to his wife. He fell to his knees at her side and hesitantly reached a visibly trembling hand to her face; he caressed her cheek and brushed her hair out of the way, doing so with a tenderness that belied the fact that he had publicly humiliated her over a spilt glass of wine just a short time before.

"Is...is she dead?" he asked in a voice that quavered and cracked and threatened to break entirely.

"No, Mr Moore, I found a pulse, she's alive," Nathan said reassuringly. "She's alive," he repeated. "She's unconscious, and obviously injured, but she is alive. Do we have a first-aider here, or someone with medical training?" he asked of those gathered in the foyer.

"I'm the hotel first-aider," a young voice said from the crowd by the dining room doors.

Nathan was careful not to say what he was thinking as a young woman, one of the waitresses, stepped forward, which was that he would have liked the first-aider to be someone older, preferably someone with more experience. Given what he could see of Helen Moore's injuries, he didn't like the thought of her being cared for by someone who looked as though the worst they had had to deal with was a papercut. He had no choice in the matter, though; since they couldn't call anyone because of the storm, they couldn't get an ambulance to come and take Helen Moore to hospital, so she had to be looked after there.

"What's your name?"

"Sally, Sally Green."

"Okay, Sally, I want you to check her over. It looks to me like she has a broken leg and an injured arm, as well being unconscious. I'd like you to assess whether she's okay to be moved, because she can't be kept here." Nathan turned to Jennifer Pierson then. "We need a room nearby, I guess it'll have to be on the first floor, where we can put her, and something we can use to move her on once Miss Green says she's okay to be moved. A stretcher would be ideal, but I don't suppose you have one lying around, so anything that can be turned into a makeshift stretcher.

"The rest of you should go back to your meals," he told the others gathered in the foyer in a voice that was loud enough that none of them could claim not to have heard him, not even those that he could see were sporting hearing aids. "I may need to speak to you later, but for now I want you all to relax as best you can. Not you, Mr Bonner," he said when he saw that the second party in the fight was about to follow the crowd into the restaurant. "Nor you, Louisa, nor you, Constable."

He didn't really need to tell his friend to stay, she had made no move to leave; similarly, Constable Havers made no attempt to depart the scene, though in his case it was because he was still unaware of what was going on.

23

With as much care as they could manage, and thankful that she was unconscious, Nathan and Constable Havers manoeuvred Helen Moore from the makeshift stretcher to the bed in the vacant first-floor room that Jennifer Pierson had found for them.

"Are you okay to stay here with Mrs Moore?" Nathan asked of Sally Green, who had followed them up to the room.

Sally nodded. "Yes, of course, I'll keep an eye on her, make sure nothing happens."

"Thank you." Why he did it, he couldn't say, but Nathan paused in the doorway as he was about to leave the room and looked back at Helen Moore. Something about her face made him return to the bed, so he could examine it more closely. "Does she look like Tracey Pierson to you?" he asked of Havers.

"I didn't notice it before, but now you mention it, I can see a resemblance," Havers said after joining his superior at the bed so he could take his own closer look at Helen Moore. "Do you think there could be some significance to the fact that Tracey Pierson and Mrs Moore look alike? You said Tracey Pierson was killed because of the affair she was having." No sooner had he said that than he thought about the need for discretion. He looked around guiltily, but soon realised that apart from Sally Green, who was paying no attention to what he said, there was no-one around to hear him.

"I did say that," Nathan agreed. "And I still believe it."

"Do you not think Mrs Moore could have been attacked by the same person who killed Tracey, and that Tracey was killed by mistake? Maybe the killer got the two of them mixed up in the dark and thought Tracey was Mrs Moore."

Nathan shook his head. "We have to check it out, we can't afford to simply ignore it, but I think it far more likely that what has happened to Mrs Moore is unrelated to Tracey Pierson's murder. Her murder is connected to the affair she was having, I'm even more convinced of that after the conversation I overheard this afternoon, when I was nearly able to make an arrest, and with a bit more work we'll prove it and catch the person responsible — the woman scorned," he said confidently. "As for Mrs Moore, I suspect we're going to find that it was an accident."

"I hope you're right, sir," Havers said fervently. "The village is going to have a hard enough time coping with one murder, a second, attempted, murder will be too much for people. We get by on our own for the most part, but we do rely on the holidaymakers, like yourself, to help us get through tougher times. Something like this could keep them away in the future, and that's likely to end with the village becoming like some sort of ghost town."

Nathan could appreciate the concern the constable had for the damage recent events could do to his village. The spirit of almost any community could be damaged by a murder, and in a place as small as Donningford that damage was likely to be more serious. The state of the community's spirit was of no concern to Nathan, though, his job was to solve the murder and catch the person responsible. What happened to the village after that was the concern of other people, for which he was more than a little relieved since he didn't have the first clue how to deal with such things.

AFTER A DETOUR TO THE kitchen, Nathan returned to the foyer with a steaming mug of hot chocolate and Constable Havers a step behind him.

As they had been instructed, he found Arthur Moore and Simon Bonner still there. They remained on either side of the reception area, eyeing one another with a mixture of wariness and animosity. It was understandable, Nathan thought, Moore blamed Bonner for what had happened to his wife, and Bonner was concerned that he was going to be attacked again.

Between the two men stood Louisa, positioned as if to keep them apart should they decide to resume hostilities. As slim as she was, it was unlikely that she would be much use if she had to try and stop a fight, not if the two men were really determined; Simon Bonner was as slim as Louisa, but Moore was twice her size and liable to run right over the top of her.

Despite the anger and animosity that filled the foyer, it didn't seem as if any blows had been struck, or even attempted. Nathan was thankful for that since it meant there was nothing new for him to deal with; he had enough to do already, he didn't want to have to deal with more.

"Mr Bonner, would you mind coming with me?" Nathan asked. "I have a few questions for you about this evening's *incident*."

"I think we should speak first, Nate," Louisa said, catching his eye.

Nathan was surprised by the mysterious tone from his friend, it wasn't like her and it made him curious. He tried to ask a question with his eyes but either he wasn't able to frame it properly or Louisa wasn't willing to clarify anything while there were people around to hear her.

"Okay, come on, we'll talk in the office," he said, hoping it was important. He was sure it was, he doubted Louisa would interrupt his investigation without a good reason. "Wait here, Mr Bonner, I'll come back for you when I've finished with Ms Orchard."

"OKAY, WHAT IS IT, LOU?" Nathan asked the moment they were alone in the office.

"That email you had me sort out," Louisa said, "it managed to get through. I guess the storm must have slacked at some point, long enough for the laptop to get a connection to the internet at least."

Nathan was pleased with that piece of news but couldn't see that it was worth cutting in on his interview with Mr Bonner. "I don't suppose there's been a reply," he said hopefully, not daring to cross his fingers, it was enough of a miracle that the email had made it through the storm.

"There has." Louisa smiled at the surprise on her friend's face. "Along with seven junk emails, which must have appeared almost the instant the laptop managed to get a signal, I had an email from my assistant and another from Stephen. How long he spent trying to get the email through I have no idea, but there was more than two hours between the time your email was sent and his was received."

Nathan didn't care about any of that, he only cared that there had been an answer. He doubted the response from Stephen would enable him to make an arrest and close his case, that would be too much to hope for, but it might bring a resolution closer, if he was lucky. Eagerly, he asked, "What did Stephen have to say?"

"I'll skip the pleasantries, you can read them for yourself later," Louisa said, sensing that Nathan wasn't interested in anything but the meat of the message. "He said he hasn't been able to find anything on the Piersons, except that they're the registered owners of The Moor's Edge hotel, have one daughter and two cars, and are originally from London. I assume he hasn't found any kind of criminal record for them, because he included a whole bunch of trivial stuff that was a little interesting but not really all that useful.

"He was able to find possibly relevant information on two of the guests: Simon Bonner and a Jody Lennox, he included pictures, so you can be sure you've got the right people — I'm surprised the email got through with pictures attached."

Nathan understood then why Louisa had wanted to speak to him before he interviewed Simon Bonner and was glad he hadn't ignored her. "What did Stephen have to say about them?"

"Jody Lennox has an arrest warrant out against him from Northumberland Police, he's wanted for skipping out on bail. He was supposed to appear in court a couple of months ago on an assault charge but never showed, they've been looking for him ever since. No known connection to any of the Piersons, but Stephen said he's looking into it." Louisa paused for a moment to give Nathan a chance to digest that. "Simon Bonner was born in Liverpool but now lives and works in Manchester; he's got a lengthy record, you name it, he's done it. Stephen included a condensed version of his rap sheet and even that takes up a fair amount of space. Apparently, it's suspected that Bonner works for the Cabot family in Manchester. I've never heard of them, but according to Stephen they're into drugs, prostitution, and loan-sharking, pretty much anything that'll make them money, but in the past decade they've apparently become semi-legit.

"What Bonner does for the Cabots, he couldn't say, but Stephen's trying to find out more. He promised to email as soon as he's got more information on any of the names we sent him. Of course, he could have sent a dozen more emails by now and we just haven't received them."

Nathan accepted that with a nod. There was no point wasting time on emails that hadn't been received, which could contain anything or nothing. Instead he focused on the information he did have.

"I've heard of the Cabots. I don't know much about them, but they've come up in conversation at conferences I've been to — the Krays, but with a thin veneer of civilisation and a semi-legit front from what I've heard. This hardly seems like the kind of place someone who works for them would come on holiday, especially when doing so finds him at the scene of a near fatal incident." The information he now had was making him revise his original opinion with regards to Helen Moore's injury. "It would help if Stephen had been able to find out something about the Moores; I'm sure Constable Havers has them down as being from Manchester as well, that can't be a coincidence."

Louisa wasn't slow on the uptake. She had known Nathan long enough to be able to follow his thinking without the need for him to say too much. "You think the Moores could be involved with the Cabots, owe them money maybe, and Bonner was sent to sort the situation out?" If she hadn't spent so long reporting on crime, in all its various aspects, she would have thought the notion better suited to a television drama or a film. Experience had taught her that no matter how far-fetched something might seem, if someone could imagine it, there was every chance it was true.

Nathan shrugged. "It's possible, but it seems unlikely. Even if Bonner is here to sort out a situation with the Moores, he'd have to be a real idiot to do anything, especially something that might lead to a death, when we're all stuck here by a storm and he knows there's a police investigation underway because of another death." Unfortunately, he knew just how stupid many criminals could be. "Was there anything else in Stephen's email?"

Louisa shook her head. "That's all he had. He did say he'll send more when he's got it. I'll keep an eye on my laptop in case something gets through," she said. "Though to judge by the noise the storm is making, I don't think anything's going to happen anytime soon. Do you want me to send Bonner in when I get back out there?" she asked, getting to her feet.

"Please, and tell Havers to come in as well, he should be here while I interview Bonner." Wrapping his hands around the mug of hot chocolate, which was cooling far too rapidly for his liking, Nathan watched his friend leave. He didn't know what it was but there was something comforting about drinking hot chocolate when the weather outside was rubbish; he wasn't cold, but he did feel a pleasant warmth spread through him as he sipped at his drink.

24

It was a couple of minutes before Simon Bonner entered the office on the heels of Constable Havers, who resigned himself to a standing position off to one side when he realised there was nowhere for him to sit once Bonner had taken the seat at the desk.

If Bonner was concerned about being questioned in connection with a death, he showed no sign of it. He sat across the desk from the inspector, looking calmer and more composed than the average person would have under the circumstances. His eyes darted around the room, taking in all there was to see, which wasn't much, before coming to rest on Nathan and assuming an intensity that would have disturbed most people.

Nathan didn't need the information from the email Stephen had sent to know that Bonner had had dealings with the police before. His demeanour made it clear that he was familiar with police procedures and personnel and had long since ceased being troubled by them. Fortunately, Nathan was as used to hardened criminals as Bonner was to the police.

A long minute passed in silence before Nathan spoke. He didn't imagine it was going to get a result on this occasion, but he liked to allow a minute or so to pass before he got started, so that if the person he was interviewing was a nervous sort they might blurt something out just to fill the silence.

"Did you know Mr Moore and his wife before you came here on holiday, Mr Bonner?" he asked finally.

Bonner shook his head. "No, never met them."

"You come from Manchester, though, same as the Moores," Nathan said. "It seems a little coincidental, don't you think?"

"Not really. What, you don't think it possible that three people from Manchester could decide to come here, to this wonderfully peaceful place, without there being a connection between them or an ulterior motive?" Bonner tried to make the idea sound ridiculous but couldn't quite pull it off.

Nathan smiled. "Under other circumstances, I might dismiss it as a coincidence, but not when one of the people in question works for the Cabot family and he was found standing over the unconscious body of one of the others, who was heard to scream before being found at the foot of the stairs. I'm sure you can understand how it must look," he said. "In all honesty, I think it unlikely that someone with a record as long and as varied as yours would be foolish enough to do anything when you know there are people in the hotel looking for a murderer. If that isn't enough to make you act sensibly, I'm sure the thought of what the Cabots would do to you if you did something so stupid would."

Bonner made no attempt to deny that he worked for the Cabot family, instead he said, "I'm sorry, but who are you to be questioning me like this? I assume you're police, given the circumstances and the way the constable is acting, but you haven't bothered to introduce yourself. I was under the impression that you're a holidaymaker, like me."

"Sorry," Nathan apologised. "I was just another holidaymaker, until Mrs Pierson's death was discovered to be something other than the accident it was originally believed to be. I'm Detective Inspector Stone." He took out his warrant card and held it out to be examined by Bonner, who spared it only the briefest of glances. "Now, as I'm sure you must realise, it isn't possible to get a solicitor here for you, unless we have one amongst the guests, so this can't be considered a formal interrogation. Nonetheless, I need some answers.

"Before we begin, why don't we simply take it for granted that you work for the Cabots and save us both the useless denials. Exactly what you do for them, I can only guess, and I don't imagine you're going to tell me. I'm not interested in what you do for them, though, not unless it has a bearing on what happened with Mrs Moore, so why don't you tell me what happened, and how you came to be found at the foot of the stairs, kneeling over her." He held up a hand to forestall what Bonner was about to say. "Before you think about lying, I think I should tell you that I'm pretty good at sniffing out bullshit, and the moment this storm is over, I'll know everything there is to know about you and the Cabots, what I don't already know that is. I'm also very good at ferreting out secrets, so good in fact that once we finish with you, Constable Havers will be arresting a young man from Northumberland who has skipped out on his bail."

Bonner's reaction to that was minimal, certainly less visible than Havers', but it was there for Nathan to see, if only because he was looking for it. Bonner had got the message, even in the middle of a crippling storm the inspector could get information that others would prefer he didn't.

"Yeah, I work for the Cabots," Bonner said, surprising Nathan with the admission since he had already said he wasn't concerned about that just then.

"What do you do for them?" Nathan asked. Since Bonner had admitted to working for the Cabots he figured he might as well find out how much the man would reveal. He guessed that he would only be told what he could find out through other sources; it was unlikely that a career criminal would reveal anything that couldn't be discovered easily.

"I work security for them."

"That doesn't seem very likely to me, Mr Bonner. Even if you ignore the fact that you lack the physique normally associated with someone working security; someone with a record like yours would never be able to pass the CRB check to get registered as a security officer, not with any properly registered agency anyway. Are the Cabots running a dodgy security agency? I'm sure the police up in Manchester would love to hear all about it." From the little he knew about the Cabots, Nathan would have expected them to be more careful than to employ ex-criminals in an agency providing security personnel; even a quick check by police would reveal the registrations weren't legitimate.

"You've got it all wrong," Bonner said quickly. "The Cabots run a legit security firm, you can check it if ya want. I don't work for the firm, though, I work directly for the Cabots as a driver and do some private security work for them, no public contact, except by accident, so there's no problem with my CRB state." A smile, which threatened to become a smug smirk, appeared briefly on his lips.

It was clever, Nathan had to admit that, a neat way of getting around the regulations, which had never been as clear-cut as he would have liked them to be. For the moment, though, the fact that the Cabots were pushing the rules on employing people with criminal records didn't matter, he had more immediate matters to deal with.

"Did you know the Moores before you came down here for your holiday?"

"No." Bonner went on quickly before Nathan could say anything, "I'd heard the name, they own a construction firm, same as the Cabots, and I've heard they're after a contract to build a new school, same as the Cabots, but that's all I know about them."

Nathan didn't believe him. Bonner was trying to conceal something, he could see it in his eyes, but he had no idea what, he assumed it was something to do with the Cabots.

"So how come both you and the Moores chose to come here on holiday?" he asked.

Bonner shrugged. "No idea. How'm I supposed to know why the Moores came here, I don't know 'em. I'm here 'cause I needed a holiday and I came here with my family when I was a kid. I don't much like foreign travel, dealing with all those foreigners and their mucky food winds me up, I much prefer the English countryside. I was reminded of this place a while back, so when I was thinking about where to go on holiday I decided to come back here."

There was a ring of truth to what Bonner said, but at the same time there was a hint in his eye that suggested he wasn't telling the whole truth.

"Okay, so you're here to relive your childhood memories," Nathan said. "Tell me how you happened to be found kneeling over Helen Moore at the foot of the stairs."

"I don't know what happened," Bonner said. "Honest, I don't. I was heading along the first floor to the stairs, so I could come down for dinner. I got to the head of the stairs just as Mrs Moore got there from the foyer. There was a flash of lightning, which must have caught her by surprise; she screamed and fell down the stairs. I tried to catch her but wasn't close enough.

"I hurried down the stairs to check on her, and that's when everyone came out from the dining room."

Nathan saw nothing in Bonner's face or body language to suggest that he was lying, but he knew he could be mistaken. "Was there anyone else around who could corroborate your story?"

Bonner shook his head. "I didn't see anyone. If there was someone around, they disappeared real quick."

"So you're saying it was an accident."

"Yeah. She musta been frightened by the lightning. Either that or it was the sight of me." Bonner shrugged, clearly not concerned by that possibility.

Nathan was silent for a few moments while he considered what he had been told. No-one had come forward with a story that contradicted Bonner's, and all he had seen when he reached the foyer was Bonner kneeling over Helen Moore's body, which wasn't enough to condemn the man as an attempted murderer, even with his criminal record.

"I may have further questions for you, Mr Bonner, once I've spoken to anyone who might have seen anything. For the time being, though, this looks like an unfortunate accident." Under other circumstances, he would have told Bonner not to leave town without notifying the police; there was little point in doing so then, however, since Bonner couldn't leave the hotel, let alone the village, even if he wanted to.

25

Nathan was in bed, looking through everything he had assembled so far, both on the murder of Tracey Pierson and on the incident involving Helen Moore.

He could feel a headache building behind one eye and hoped it was the result of him reading by the dim light of the lamp on the bedside table, or the lateness of the hour, rather than the pressure of the situation. He wasn't normally affected by the pressure of an investigation, but the circumstances just then were a little unusual.

Rubbing his tired eyes for a moment, Nathan leant over to lay the sheet of paper he had just finished reading on top of the stack that sat on the floor next to the bed. He then picked up the glass from the bedside table, so he could sip at his water for a few moments, before returning to his reading.

He wasn't having much success in finding anything useful in the statements taken by Constable Havers, or in the printouts Louisa had produced from Tracey Pierson's computer, but he wasn't going to have any better luck by giving up. Nothing in what he had read so far helped him to identify either the man Tracey Pierson was having an affair with or his wife.

Nathan was tempted to eliminate all the non-single women who were on the list of guests; that would reduce his number of suspects to just three, and of those three, one was an elderly woman who didn't look capable of lifting the tenderiser used as a murder weapon, light as it was, let alone striking a fatal blow with it, while the second was the mousy, librarian-looking Elizabeth Creek, who seemed too meek to attack anyone.

He was on the verge of taking out the statements from the three single women and putting aside the others when he realised what a stupid idea it was. He knew virtually nothing about the woman he believed was responsible for the murder, not what she looked like, nor the name she had registered at the hotel with.

He couldn't eliminate any of the women until he found out more about the mysterious Laura, whom he had heard arguing with the husband who had left her. For all he knew, she had come to the hotel with someone who was completely unaware of her reason for being there.

The storm, which continued to rage outside — it was all he could do to concentrate with the wind howling and the rain lashing against the window — was a double-edged sword, Nathan decided. On the one hand it prevented the killer getting away before she was identified, but on the other it left him cut off from any of the help, especially forensic expertise, that might make the difference between catching the killer and not.

Louisa might believe that he preferred old-school policing to more modern techniques, and she might even be right, he reflected, but even old-school detectives had had the use of fingerprints and access to police and other records to help them solve cases.

No matter how much he read of the material gathered so far, he couldn't get past the central facts: Tracey Pierson had been having an affair; her lover was either separated or divorced from his wife; the wife knew of her husband's affair and knew who the affair was with, and the wife had threatened Tracey Pierson with exposure of the affair if she didn't end it. Most importantly, the wife, whose first name he knew to be Laura, was at the hotel, had been recognised by her husband,

and overheard by both himself and Jennifer Pierson admitting to the murder.

Nathan was confident that he could prove a case against the murderer, once he caught her. It was catching her that was proving difficult, and it was likely to remain that way until he could get in contact with Stephen without lengthy delays and prayers for the storm to abate.

There was always the possibility that he would get lucky and something would fall into his lap that would enable him to make an arrest before the storm passed, but in his current mood he didn't feel confident of that.

He had decided to give his eyes a break and get some rest, and was about to turn off the lamp, so he could do that, when a thought occurred to him. Hanging halfway out of the single bed, Nathan groped around the floor under him until his hand finally closed around the sealed evidence bag containing the murder weapon. The CPS was likely to have a collective fit if they discovered he had such a crucial piece of evidence under his bed, rather than having it locked up securely, but circumstances left him with few choices.

With a groan for the effort, he righted himself, bringing the plastic-wrapped tenderiser to his lap, where it sat for a moment, while he recovered from the dizzying manoeuvre.

Had there been anyone in the room to ask what he was up to, Nathan doubted he would have been able to come up with a satisfactory answer. All he knew was that he hadn't yet taken a proper look at the weapon used to murder Tracey Pierson, and his instincts were telling him that he should.

The head of the tenderiser revealed nothing, except for the blood and hair that clung to its rough surface, proving that it was the item used to commit murder. Nor was there anything on the handle, at least nothing that was visible at first glance. A second, more intent, look revealed something that he had missed the first time and he reached for the lamp to tilt the shade up, so he could shine the light directly onto the handle of the tenderiser. He then leant forward to examine the scratches he had discovered closer.

Initially they looked like a simple series of scratches, the kind that might have resulted from indifferent handling, but something told him that this was an implement that was treated carefully by its owner. Whether the owner was male or female was uncertain, but Nathan didn't think they would have let it get scratched by accident.

After examining the tenderiser as closely as he could, even going so far as to squint and strain his eyes, he decided that the scratches were letters. It took a little longer before he felt confident in saying that the letters were an S and an M, and that they were the initials of the murder weapon's owner. The only problem he had with his conclusion was that he could think of no-one, either among the guests or the staff, who had those initials.

That left him perplexed, especially since he was sure the tenderiser belonged to someone who worked in the hotel's kitchen. It wasn't the sort of thing a person would carry around randomly.

Finally, Nathan gave up trying to puzzle it out. He might have better luck in the morning, he decided, when he was fresher and more awake. He returned the vital piece of evidence to its place of safety under the bed — he chuckled to himself at that — scribbled the initials on a scrap of paper, and then turned out the light so he could get some sleep.

26

Nathan yawned hugely as he slowly descended the stairs, his eyes half-closed and his arms reaching for the ceiling as he stretched to ease muscles gone stiff through sleep. He stepped off the last stair and into the foyer in time for his stomach to grumble loudly in response to the smell of breakfast that wafted out from the dining room.

Ignoring the demands of his stomach, he made his way down the passage, past the dining room, and into the kitchen at the rear of the hotel. He stopped in the doorway and looked around; he saw two cooks, busy preparing bacon, eggs, toast, tomatoes, baked beans, and whatever else the hungry guests might want, and two waitresses, plus Jennifer Pierson, who were in and out of the kitchen, collecting plates of food to take through to the dining room.

He couldn't be certain, but Nathan thought there was supposed to be three cooks. He assumed the third, if he wasn't imagining him, was having the breakfast off due to it being less demanding than either lunch or dinner.

Nathan's first thought was to wait until breakfast was over before getting on with what he was there for. He couldn't bring himself to wait, however. Despite the perfectly sensible explanation he had thought of for why the third cook wasn't there, he couldn't help feeling that there was another reason, one that wasn't quite so innocent.

Waiting was not going to make him appear, he was sure of that, though he couldn't have said how he knew that, except by instinct.

"Excuse me, everyone. Excuse me." Nathan lifted his voice to be heard above the noise of cooking. "Any of you recognise this?" he asked once he had the attention of those in the kitchen. He lifted the bag containing the murder weapon, so it could be seen by everyone.

"It's a tenderiser," one of the cook's said, a hint of sarcasm in his voice, as both cooks, Jennifer Pierson and the waitress who had just entered the kitchen looked over to see who had spoken and what they were supposed to be recognising.

"Strangely enough, I already knew it was a tenderiser," Nathan said, leaving the doorway so he could approach the young man, who couldn't have been much more than twenty-one. The bacon spat at him as he passed but he ignored it, sure that there was nothing personal behind the attack, it was just bacon being bacon, the smell of which made his stomach rumble. "I was hoping that one of you might have seen this particular tenderiser before. You see, this tenderiser is the item used to kill Jennifer's mother, and it has some initials scratched into the end of the handle, an S and an M. I'm hoping one of you can tell me who it belongs to." He held the bag out for closer scrutiny.

"An S and an M?" Jennifer asked, puzzled, as she walked around the counter where she had been waiting for the next couple of plates to be sorted. When she reached Nathan, she took the evidence bag from him, so she could examine the instrument that had robbed her of her mother. "It's a J, not an S," she said when she was done with her scrutiny.

"A J?" Nathan asked. He didn't think he would have concluded that the first of the two letters scratched into the metal was a J no matter how much time he spent examining it, it had to be the worst J he had ever seen. "Are you sure?"

"Uh huh." Jennifer nodded. She crossed to where a gleaming set of knives hung from a magnetic strip that was fixed to the wall and took one down. "See, J and M," she said, showing Nathan the letters scratched badly into the handle. "Jean Martin. He's marked all his stuff the same, so no-one will make the mistake of using them he says. They're expensive and only to be used by a professional chef, not a mere cook, or worse, an amateur.

"He's terrible when it comes to engraving, and his handwriting with a pen isn't much better, but he is a really good chef, close to brilliant. Beyond brilliant to hear him talk. I'd wonder how mum and dad persuaded him to come and work here, but I think he just likes to play the part of the big-shot chef to wind people up. He especially likes to wind these two up." Jennifer indicated the two listening cooks. "He studied at some fancy culinary school, while they only went to a regular college to learn the essentials. You don't think Jean killed mum, do you?" she asked suddenly as the thought occurred to her. "He wouldn't do that. I don't think he'd ever hurt anyone, for any reason."

"No, I don't think he killed your mum," Nathan said. "But I do think there might be some significance to the fact that an item of his was used as the murder weapon, and I'm curious to know why he didn't report this missing, or at least mention its absence. I assume none of you were aware that Mr Martin had lost his tenderiser." The last was directed at the cooks and the waitresses, both of whom were now in the kitchen.

"No." It was the same cook who had spoken before who answered, while his companion nodded his agreement. "He must not have known it was missing, he doesn't use it much. He'd have raised holy hell if he knew."

Nathan could think of another reason why Jean Martin hadn't kicked up a stink over the missing tenderiser — he had guessed why it had gone missing and who had taken it and didn't want to be connected to the situation. Most likely he had hoped that the tenderiser would never be connected to him, and that his involvement with Tracey Pierson would not be discovered.

"Do any of you know where Jean Martin is right now?"

Jennifer shrugged. "At a guess, I'd say he's up in his room. As far as he's concerned, breakfast is beneath someone of his talents, he almost never helps out. He does lunch and dinner, things that require skill. He'll come down in time to make the soups, not before."

"You'd better show me to his room," Nathan said. He had a bad feeling, though he couldn't have said what had caused it. "I need to speak to him about his tenderiser, amongst other things."

NATHAN AND JENNIFER reached the room used by Jean Martin in just a couple of minutes, and when they got there Nathan knocked loudly and called out.

"Mr Martin, it's Inspector Stone, open up please, I need to ask you some questions."

When there was no response after half a minute, Nathan knocked again and then tried the door handle. The door was locked, which he supposed could mean the chef was somewhere else in the hotel, occupying himself in some way before he started work, but some instinct told him that something was wrong.

"Have you got a spare key for this door?" Nathan asked, rattling the door handle again before dropping to one knee to press an eye to the keyhole in the hope of seeing something of the room. He had no luck for something, the key he assumed, was in the lock, preventing him seeing anything.

"Uh huh," Jennifer said with a nod. "Dad's got it, though, I'll have to go and get it. Do you want to stay here or come with me?"

"I'll stay here," Nathan told her after thinking for a few moments. "It's possible that Mr Martin is trying to avoid me and will consider making a run for it when he thinks I'm gone." Where the chef might try and run to, he didn't know; the storm might have slacked off during the night, making an escape from the hotel possible, if not advisable, but it was unlikely that anyone would be able to get out of the village.

It took Jennifer less than ten minutes to return with the master keys from her dad. She sorted through them quickly for the right one, but when she tried it in the lock she couldn't get the door to open. To begin with she thought it was because she had the wrong key, but after trying several others and rechecking the first one she had picked she stared at the lock, puzzled.

"That's odd," she said when she finally admitted defeat. "If the door's only been locked, the key should pop out when I put mine in, it's not, though. Either Jean's turned the key in the lock, so it can't be pushed out, or the lock's been jammed somehow."

"Maybe Mr Martin wanted to make sure that no-one could get in while he was sleeping," Nathan suggested. "If he is the person your mother was having an affair with, and one of the people we heard having an argument yesterday — the woman, Laura, called the man John, at least that's what we thought, she could have been saying Jean — he might have been worried that his ex-wife would try to kill him while he slept. Of course, that doesn't explain why he hasn't responded to our efforts to get his attention.

"Under the circumstances, I think it best if I force the door. Do you have any objections?"

Nathan could see that Jennifer was uncertain about him breaking the door down. She said nothing against it, though, so he put his shoulder to the door, which didn't move. He tried again, with the same lack of success. It quickly became apparent that when it came to a contest between his shoulder and the solid wood of the door, his shoulder was going to lose; he could already feel a bruise forming, the size of which he didn't want to think about.

Since his shoulder was no use, and there was no space for him to get a decent run-up, which would have enabled him to use his whole weight against the door, he decided to resort to other methods. His first kick left a footprint on the white paint of the door, his second made the door shudder, and the third shattered the lock.

Splinters flew as the door burst open to bang against the wall before bouncing back, forcing Nathan to thrust a hand out quickly to keep it from hitting him in the face.

He stopped almost as soon as he crossed the threshold, annoyed, and deeply unhappy, to see that he had been left with another problem to deal with.

Jennifer entered the room on Nathan's heels, though she had to stop almost immediately as Nathan halted, forcing her to lean around him so she could see the room. Her eyes were drawn to the bed and what it held but she immediately spun away, her stomach heaving as she fought the urge to throw up.

It wasn't that she could see much, except for the handle of the knife and a small red stain, but the knowledge of what she wasn't quite seeing was enough to make her nauseous.

"Is he...is he dead?" she asked in a hesitant voice, afraid that the mere act of talking would be enough to make her lose control.

Nathan could guess at the answer, based on what he could see, nonetheless he moved forward and shifted the pillow out of the way, so he could press his fingers to Jean Martin's throat. A single touch was enough to confirm what his eyes had already told him; the chef had been dead for some time, hours, he could only guess at how many, but even being covered up hadn't helped to keep his body warm. He was as cold as only a dead person could be.

"He's dead," he said with a sad nod as he looked down at the deceased man. He realised that it was irrational, but he couldn't help feeling that the murder was his fault; if he had been cleverer and quicker he would have linked the tenderiser to Martin yesterday, and by doing so he could perhaps have prevented him being killed. "Damn," he swore briefly, venting his emotions before turning to Jennifer. "When you feel up to it, would you mind finding Constable Havers and bringing him here?"

Jennifer nodded weakly and left the room. She was glad to be away from the body of the man she had known for the past two years, but she didn't think she would be able to forget the look on his face that had been revealed when the pillow was taken away. She stumbled down the passage towards the stairs, and as she did so she wondered how life could have changed so dramatically for her in such a short time.

Her life had not been perfect — her parents' marriage had been coming apart, and her father had been doing everything he could to keep her from having the life she wanted — but it had been good more than it had been bad. Now, though, her mother was dead, her father was torn between grief over her death and anger over the discovery that she had been having an affair, a guest had suffered a serious injury, and the man her mother had most likely been having an affair with had been murdered.

For an eighteen-year-old it was too much, especially since she was having to do her best to run the hotel while her father wallowed in his emotions.

If anyone had troubled to ask him, Nathan was sure he could have made a reasonably accurate guess as to what was on Jennifer Pierson's mind. The teen's troubles, serious though they might be for her, didn't concern him just then, though, he had more important things to worry about, like catching a killer before she could strike for a third time. That caused a nasty little thought to pop into his mind, one that once there he couldn't get rid of.

Simon Bonner had said that Helen Moore's fall was an accident, the result of a scare brought on by a sudden flash of lightning, but now he couldn't help wondering if it might not instead have somehow been the work of Jean Martin's estranged and seemingly deranged wife.

It was possible, he thought, that Helen Moore had seen or heard something which could identify Laura Martin under the identity she was using while at the hotel. If Laura Martin had discovered that there was someone who could identify her, it seemed likely that she would have killed to keep her secret.

The murder of Tracey Pierson may well have been an irritational act, but the attempt afterward to make it look like a tragic but accidental fall in the woods smacked of cold and calculating behaviour. Not to mention the attempt to frame him once it had been discovered that Tracey Pierson had been murdered.

Anyone who was prepared to go to the effort that Laura Martin had was surely prepared to commit murder a second, or even a third, time to keep from being caught, as demonstrated by the sight before him.

Why Simon Bonner would say Helen Moore had fallen if there had been an attempt to kill her, and he wasn't responsible, Nathan had no idea. Since there was no good reason for Bonner to do so, it made it unlikely that he would have. Thinking that, Nathan put aside the possibility that he was dealing with an attempted murder on top of two actual murders, though he knew it was something he would have to look into later. Just then he had the body of Jean Martin to deal with.

Although he didn't know exactly who had stuck a pillow over the chef's head and a knife through his heart, he did know who Jean Martin's killer was. All he had to do was figure out what name Laura Martin was using and what she looked like.

The lessening of the storm, which had only a fraction of the intensity it had possessed when he went to sleep, gave him hope that he would once again be able to contact the outside world. If he could manage that there was every chance that he would be able to close his case that day, a possibility that lifted his spirits, which had been flagging in the face of the storm and the murders.

Having thought of that possibility, he reached into his pocket for his mobile phone. A glance at the screen revealed that he had a signal, only one bar in strength, half what he had been able to get before the storm, but infinitely better than no bars. He immediately hit the speed dial button for Stephen and crossed his fingers.

When he heard the dial tone, followed by the ringing of the phone at the other end, Nathan allowed himself a brief prayer of thanks, even though he wasn't religious.

"Stephen, it's Nathan," he said needlessly when his call was answered, he had never known his friend to answer the phone without first checking the screen to see who was calling.

"Nathan, bloody hell, don't tell me that storm has finally released you."

It was amazing, Nathan thought, how much of a relief it could be to hear the voice of a friend. It was one thing to not speak to someone out of choice, that was easy to tolerate, but to need to speak to someone and not be able to because of something out of his control was almost intolerable.

"Not quite yet," Nathan told his friend. "It's loosened its grip, but it hasn't let go yet."

"I've been keeping an eye on the weather reports for down there, looks like you've had it rough." Stephen shook his head, to the amusement of those in the CID offices with him. "A storm on one side and a murderer on the other. Rather you than me. Collins told me you got roped in to handle the investigation because the storm is keeping the locals away."

Nathan had to smile at that, though he found little humour in the situation. "Something like that. From what I've been told, it's going to be at least a few days after the storm finally stops before access to the village is restored, so I could be late back from this holiday. Mind you, we have been lucky; apparently, it's a pretty common occurrence during storms like this to lose power. At least we've managed to avoid that."

"Thank god that didn't happen. I've got to say, it sounds like you've been stuck in the middle of a nineteen-forties or fifties noir detective movie."

"Lou described it as an Agatha Christie novel, with me as a poor man's Poirot." It didn't make Nathan feel any better about the situation to have another of his friends describe it in a similar fashion.

"That might be going a bit far," Stephen remarked. "I suppose you're calling because you want the rest of the information Louisa emailed me for." He had been standing in the main office of Branton Police Station's CID section, but now he made for the office he shared with Nathan, so he could get the information from his computer.

"No, I've got something else I need at the moment," Nathan told his friend. "I'm standing over a second murder victim as we speak, goes by the name of Jean Martin, that's the French Jean, not the English John, a chef. I believe it's his ex-wife, estranged wife, I'm not sure what she is, who killed him. She held a pillow over his face and stabbed him through the heart. I've got maybe two days before people can get out of the village again. If I can't identify her by then, she might get away with it."

"Okay, don't worry, I'll find out who she is for you," Stephen said. "I'll get looking straight away, but anything you can get me on this Jean Martin will make it easier for me."

Nathan felt a weight lift from his shoulders as he ended the call and slipped the phone into his pocket. It might take some time for Stephen to get the information he was after, nonetheless he was confident that he would get it soon enough, enabling him to make an arrest and bring an end to the case.

27

Nathan had not long finished his conversation with Stephen when Jennifer returned with Constable Havers. He heard them before they reached the door, enabling him to stop them from entering the room and further contaminating the crime scene.

"Thank you, Jennifer, would you mind finding my friend, Louisa, now?" he asked, hoping that another errand would help to keep her mind off what she had seen in the room. "Tell her I'd like her to bring her camera, I'm going to need it."

"Jennifer said you've found the person Tracey was having an affair with, one of the cooks," Havers said once Nathan was finished with Jennifer. "She also said he's been murdered. Is that true?"

Nathan nodded. "You can see for yourself. He's been stabbed, and possibly suffocated as well." He stepped aside so Havers could enter the small room and then shut the door behind him, to keep anyone who might pass the room from seeing the body. "I'm guessing it's his wife, ex-wife — he wished he knew what the exact nature of their relationship was, not knowing irritated him — who killed him."

"The same one you think killed Tracey?"

"Uh huh." Nathan nodded. "It makes sense. She killed Tracey because of the affair, and then killed Jean here because he wouldn't agree to go back to her. Maybe it was because she couldn't have him and didn't want anyone else to have him, or maybe she was afraid he would tell us who she was." He shrugged indifferently. "The motive doesn't really bother me right now, what does is finding Jean Martin's wife. We need to figure out what name she's using and catch her before the way out of the village is clear and she gets away."

"How do you figure on catching her?" Havers wanted to know, admitting, without really wanting to, that he didn't have the first clue himself.

Nathan offered the merest hint of a smile. "We've got three chances, as I see it. Either my partner will get back to me with a name and a picture, we'll find something amongst Mr Martin's stuff to help us find her, or she'll do something stupid and give herself away. Personally, I don't think there's much chance of that last happening, she's been clever enough up to now to avoid giving herself away, which means it's down to the other two possibilities.

"Once Louisa gets here with her camera we'll photograph the scene, make sure we've got everything recorded just as it is. Then we'll take Mr Martin down to the freezer and find some room for him. I know it's not ideal," he said quickly, seeing the look on Havers' face, "but the freezer's the only place we can keep the body until it can be taken for post-mortem. After that we'll make a search of the room, focusing on paperwork and photographs. There's bound to be something here that will help us identify our killer.

"While we're doing that I'm going to have Jennifer and Louisa gather everyone in the dining room and keep them there. I've got a feeling we're going to be making an arrest today and I don't want to have to worry about where our killer's gone. Plus, if she's stuck in the middle of a crowd she's less likely to try and kill anyone else to get away."

IT TOOK BARELY A MINUTE to photograph the body of Jean Martin and the rest of the room, and that was with Nathan taking care to be sure he had captured everything that might be important. When he was done with that he began a careful examination of the room.

Since he was already ninety-nine percent certain who had killed Jean Martin, what he was most interested in discovering was how the murderer had managed to lock the door from the inside and escape. The window was closed securely, and only someone with no regard for their own safety would have tried to escape that way while the storm was still blowing.

The mystery was so perplexing that Nathan couldn't help thinking about the TV show, Jonathan Creek, from his younger years, in which a creator of illusions for a stage magician helped to solve seemingly impossible mysteries, frequently murders in locked rooms. He could do with help from someone like that just then.

"Come on then, constable." Nathan turned to Havers. "Now's your chance to shine. How did she get in here, kill Mr Martin, and get out again, all while the door was locked from the inside?"

Havers face screwed up in concentration as he tried to puzzle his way through the mystery. Finally, he had to shake his head and admit defeat. "No idea, sir," he said. "It isn't possible, is it? All I can think is that the door wasn't locked when she came in, but that doesn't explain how she got out. You had to kick the door open, so it was definitely locked. How did she do it?" He was more than a little curious to know how the seemingly impossible had been achieved.

"I'm just as stumped as you are," Nathan admitted. "I did come to the same conclusion as you, that the door wasn't locked when she arrived, either that or Mr Martin knew his murderer, which would make sense if it was his wife/ex-wife, and let them in. Unfortunately, like you, I have no idea how she got out after locking the door." He sighed irritably. "I'm sure once we figure it out we'll kick ourselves for not doing so sooner. We can worry about it another time, though. Right now, we need to start going through the room for anything that will identify his wife, and anything that will tell us who killed him, just in case it wasn't his wife."

The room was not large, it was about halfway between a single and one of the doubles, which gave Nathan some hope that if Jean Martin did have something that would identify his wife, it wouldn't take long to find it. He looked around for a moment, trying to decide where to start, and then got to work, while ignoring the mystery of the locked door, which kept trying to intrude on his thoughts.

28

Jennifer followed on Louisa's heels as the two of them hurried along the fourth-floor passage to the room Nathan and Constable Havers were searching.

"She can't have gone outside," Jennifer said in a voice that lacked certainty. "That'd be crazy. She's got to be hiding somewhere in the hotel. All we need to do is look for her."

"We have looked for her," Louisa said, neither slowing nor looking over her shoulder. "If she's hiding, she's doing a good job of it. Whether she's still here or has fled, we need to tell Nathan, so he can get the search for her organised."

Nathan appeared in the doorway of the room, drawn by the voices from the passage. "What's going on?" he asked. "Who's missing?"

Louisa scowled. "You've got the ears of a bat, Nate, anyone ever tell you that?" She wasn't really surprised that he had heard them for they weren't being quiet, and there were no other noises nearby to drown them out. "It's Elizabeth Creek, she was around for breakfast, one of the waitresses remembers serving her, but she's nowhere to be found now. Jennifer and I have checked her room and made a quick search of the hotel — she's gone. She could be hiding, or she could have fled, gone out into the storm. I know, she'd have to be crazy to try and make a run for it; the storm's died down from what it was but it's still nasty out there."

"Could this be a coincidence?" Nathan asked. He was reluctant to put a hold on his search of Jean Martin's room, especially since he hadn't yet found anything truly useful in identifying Jean Martin's wife, to go looking for someone who might not be the murderer he was after. "Is there any reason for thinking that Elizabeth Creek is our killer?"

"Some. She's booked in under the name Elizabeth Creek, and she paid with a credit card in that name, but when we checked her room after she didn't turn up when we were getting everyone into the dining room we found a bank card on the floor. It must have fallen out of her handbag when she was packing, which she clearly did in a hurry. It's in the name of Laura Dennings."

"That's the name on the divorce papers we found," Havers said from behind Nathan. He was still in the room, but as close to the doorway as he could get, so he could be included in the conversation. "It's got to be her."

"Thank you, constable," Nathan said over his shoulder. He was far from grateful for the unnecessary interruption. "I had already realised that for myself." He turned his attention back to Louisa and Jennifer, so he could focus on what was important. "How much of a search have you made?"

"Only a brief one, so far," Jennifer admitted.

"When we didn't find her in her room," Louisa said. "We checked all the passages and public areas of the hotel, then we spoke to the other guests and staff, in case any of them knew where she was. No-one's seen her since she left the dining room after breakfast. Wherever she's gone, she should have been seen by someone, this place isn't that big."

"It's big enough," Nathan remarked, before quickly shaking off his own negativity. "She'd be taking her life into her hands to go out into the storm, even if it has calmed down some. You'd better put in a call to the local search and rescue, though," he said over his shoulder to Havers. "If she's not in the hotel, they'll have the best chance of finding her. Do you think your partner will be able to get through this to help out?"

Havers crossed to the window so he could look outside before he answered. With a nod he said, "He won't like it, but yeah, he should be able to get here alright. The thunder and lightning are gone, so now it's just wind and rain to worry about, and even the wind's died down a lot from what it was. I'll get him to stop at the station on his way past and grab the emergency gear; if Elizabeth Creek/ Laura Dennings, or whatever her name is, isn't in the hotel, we're going to need it to look for her."

Nathan nodded approvingly. "Good thinking, though I sincerely hope she hasn't gone out there." His knowledge of search and rescue operations was severely limited, to the point of being all but non-existent, and he really hoped it wasn't going to come to that. Though he tried not to think about it, he worried that a search through the tail-end of a storm for a missing murderer was likely to end with either her or one of them dead or badly injured.

29

Ten minutes after Louisa and Jennifer arrived at the room where the body of Jean Martin lay, a small group assembled in the hotel's foyer.

Nathan looked around the members of the search party and wished he had been able to get more people. He also wished that he didn't have to rely so heavily on civilians for help. The hotel was not huge, at best it could be considered small to medium, but there were safety issues that had to be considered in addition to everything else; they were, after all, looking for a suspected murderer.

The last thing he wanted was to have someone, especially a civilian, hurt because they had come across Elizabeth Creek/ Laura Dennings without sufficient support.

"Okay everyone, I want you to listen up." Nathan was careful to keep his voice soft enough not to be heard by the guests in the dining room, while being loud enough to be heard by everyone in the foyer. He suspected that his discretion was a waste of time, and that most of the guests already had some idea of what was going on, but that didn't mean he should be incautious. "As I understand it, there are four exits out of this hotel: the main doors behind me, the back door which leads out to the car park from the kitchen, the fire doors at the side of the hotel, and the door which leads through to your house." He looked to Jennifer and her father for confirmation.

David Pierson nodded. "That's right. You can get out through the windows as well, but I wouldn't want to do that with the way the weather is." He spoke slowly and carefully, having drunk more than was good for him last night. "I've got all the doors locked and only myself and Jenny have the keys, so she shouldn't be able to get out without us knowing about it."

"That's great, good thinking," Nathan said. "Now, I want people at every door, two here to watch the door and the stairs, and one at each of the other doors. Whichever of you takes those positions, I don't want you to try and tackle her if you see her unless you can't avoid it, she's dangerous and may well be armed. Yell out, loud enough to be heard. That's all I want you to do if you see her." He didn't want anyone playing the hero and getting hurt. "Constables Havers and Fulton will be coming with me and Louisa to conduct the search. I'd like you and your father to stay here in reception, Jenny. You two," his gaze went to the cooks, who had agreed to help out, "will cover the rear door and the side fire exit, you can decide between yourselves which one of you goes where."

Both cooks nodded with an eagerness that disturbed Nathan. He suspected that should they come face to face with Laura Dennings they would ignore his instructions and attempt to stop her, with the hope of making a citizens' arrest. He had warned them not to, so if they got hurt they would only have themselves to blame, and short of replacing them, which he couldn't do since he was already lacking help, there was nothing he could do.

"And Miss Foster," Nathan put aside his worries about the cooks and focused on the middle-aged head of housekeeping, "will take the door to the Pierson's house." He had chosen to put her there because if Elizabeth Creek/ Laura Dennings did try and make a break for it, through the Piersons' house was the least likely direction for her to take. "Okay, if everyone knows what they're doing, let's get going. We're not going to find her standing around like this."

While the staff left to take up their assigned watch positions, Nathan, Louisa, and the two constables split up to begin the search.

Havers and his fellow constable took the ground floor, checking each room and cupboard for the missing woman, and for possible hiding places, not that they found many that were big enough for a person to squeeze into. The cellar beneath the hotel offered more opportunities for a person to hide, but if it wasn't for the electric lighting that was modern enough to leave few shadowy corners there was every chance the constables would have chickened out of going down there.

Had he known how unhappy the two constables were with searching for a murderer in the cellar, and how keen they were to get it done quickly and get out of there, Nathan would have elected to handle the search of that area himself. Since he didn't know, he continued with his search of the first floor with Louisa at his side.

The ring of spare keys that Jennifer had supplied enabled them to access every room without problems, and while Louisa remained in the doorway to keep an eye on the passage, Nathan entered each room to make a search. The single rooms had only two hiding places: under the bed and in the wardrobe, while the double rooms had three — the en-suite bathrooms had to be checked as well. Because of that it took only a few seconds to go through each room, single or double, and the pair were soon on their way up to the second floor.

NATHAN WAS ON HIS HANDS and knees, checking under the bed in room twenty-three on the second floor, Louisa's room, when the sound of hasty footsteps brought him to his feet.

He made it to the door in time to see Sally Green, the hotel's first-aider, who was supposed to be watching over Helen Moore, hurry up. The sight of her sent a stab of panic through him as he worried that her arrival meant something had happened to Helen.

"What is it?" he asked.

"Mrs Moore has woken up," Sally Green blurted out as she came to a stop.

"Well that's good news," Nathan said, relieved. He felt his panic ebb away. He was glad that he didn't have another dead body to deal with, he wasn't sure he could cope with that. "Can she talk?"

"She's a bit groggy but seems lucid."

Nathan was reluctant to abandon or pause his search for Laura Dennings, but he needed to know what had happened with Helen Moore, whether her fall was an accident or the result of an attempt on her life. He allowed himself the luxury of a few seconds to think about what he was going to do before coming to a decision.

"Can you head on back and keep an eye on her?" he requested. "I'll be there to speak to her shortly." He watched the first-aider head back down the passage to the stairs and then turned to Louisa. "Can you wait by the stairs, watch out to be sure Laura Dennings, if she's around, doesn't make a break for it? I don't want to have to search the same rooms again for her."

Less than five minutes after hearing that Helen Moore had woken, Nathan was at the first-floor room she had been placed in. He wasn't sure about leaving Louisa on her own to watch the stairs and the second floor, he hoped she wouldn't get hurt, but he wasn't confident that she would have more sense than to tangle with the murderous Laura Dennings if she were to make a break for it.

"Hello, Mrs Moore, how are you feeling?" Nathan gave a smile. "Scratch that, stupid question. I'm sure you're feeling pretty rubbish, especially since you've got a broken leg that hasn't been set. I don't know if you remember much from yesterday; in case you don't, let me introduce myself, I am Detective Inspector Nathan Stone, I'm a guest here, like yourself, on holiday, but I've been asked to take over the investigation into Tracey Pierson's murder because of the storm."

"I remember, people were talking about it, about you taking over the investigation, before dinner. Most of them were glad to hear that a detective had taken over the case."

"That's good to know," Nathan said. "Now, do you feel up to answering a few questions?"

Helen Moore nodded slowly after a few moments. "I'll do my best."

"Thank you. Okay, first and most important, what happened to you yesterday evening? Do you remember?"

Helen Moore flushed embarrassedly. "Yes, I remember. I was heading up the stairs after...after I dropped my glass and spilt wine over myself. I made it to the top of the stairs at the first floor when there was a flash of lightning, it was blinding, and this figure appeared in front of me. I don't know who it was, I didn't see them clearly; one moment there was no-one there and the next there was. It startled me and I jumped, I think I screamed as well. I lost my balance and fell.

"I don't remember anything after that, not until I woke up here."

"So, it was just an accident, you weren't pushed?" Nathan asked. "There was some concern that this was an attempt on your life, that you saw, heard, or knew something connected to the murder of Tracey Pierson."

"No, just an accident," Helen Moore said. "Just me getting scared over something silly. It's not the first time it's happened, Arthur will tell you, I've been known to jump at my own shadow."

"That's a relief, an accident is better than you being attacked," Nathan said. "That being the case, I hope you won't mind if..." Before he could finish his sentence, he was interrupted by the radio in his pocket, which squawked into life. "Sorry, would you excuse me." Getting to his feet he stepped out of the room, so he could take the radio call in the passage.

30

"Stone, have you found her?" he asked. There was no need for him to ask who was on the other end of the radio call, it could only be one of the two constables, they were the only other people in the village with radios.

"Cellar!"

The single word was gasped out by a voice that was in pain, a lot of pain. Nathan didn't know the source of the pain, or even which of the two constables was in pain, but that didn't matter just then, what did was that someone was injured, presumably in the cellar.

He could only think of two possible reasons for one of the constables to be injured, either he had been attacked by Elizabeth Creek/ Laura Dennings or there had been an accident. He suspected the former, though he had to admit that neither possibility was good, especially since there had been only one brief communication from one constable, and nothing from the other.

Leaving Sally Green to continue keeping an eye on Helen Moore, just in case there was more to her injuries than there seemed, Nathan hurried along the passage to the stairs. He made repeated efforts to contact either Constable Havers or Constable Fulton, but gave up before he reached the ground floor, when it became clear he was not going to have any luck.

The lack of communication made him increase the speed of his descent until he almost fell. He caught hold of the bannister to keep himself upright and then jumped the last half dozen stairs, landing heavily but in better shape than if he had fallen — an image of Helen Moore, and the result of her fall down those stairs, flashed through his mind.

"Cellar," he gasped as he righted himself. "Where is it?" he asked of David Pierson. He didn't wait for an answer, instead he crossed the foyer, pushed open the doors to the left and hurried over to the bar, where he guessed the door was located. If he was wrong, he was sure it had to be somewhere nearby.

"It's this way," Pierson said, catching up to the inspector and leading him past the bar and round the back to where a door stood partially open. He didn't know what was going on, but the urgency in Nathan's voice and body language kept him from asking questions; as serious as it seemed, he wasn't sure he wanted to know what had happened. His mental state was already teetering on the edge of collapse after the events of the past few days and he had no desire to make it worse. "You'll need the lights," he said. "It's like the black hole of Calcutta down there."

Nathan couldn't help the smile that lifted the corner of his mouth, he had no idea how long it had been since he last heard that phrase, but he was momentarily catapulted back to his childhood and the occasion when he had got stuck in the loft with his sister.

The light switch was on a panel to one side of the door and Pierson reached out to flip the switch. He did so several times before giving up with a puzzled expression on his face. "Something's wrong," he said unnecessarily. "The light was working fine last night when I changed a barrel, and the bulbs were changed not that long ago. Just last month I think it was, so it can't be that."

Nathan didn't like it. He had been worried enough following the single-word radio message. Discovering that the lights were out in the cellar only deepened his unease. He guessed that the two constables had encountered the missing murderess while searching the cellar, but could only imagine what had happened, something he didn't want to do. He didn't think they would have been stupid enough to go down there if the cellar had been in darkness when they got there. Doing that would have been stupid.

"Have you got any torches?" he asked of Pierson without taking his eyes from the dark doorway.

Pierson nodded. "Of course. With storms like these, torches are essential." He disappeared for a few moments before returning with a pair of heavy-duty torches. When he turned them on they emitted powerful beams of white light that were almost strong enough to blind a person, as nearly happened when Pierson passed the torches to Nathan.

Nathan accepted one of the torches and returned the other to David, who looked from it to Nathan with curiosity and concern, clearly not sure why he had a torch.

"Are there any other ways out of the cellar?"

"There's the delivery hatch, but it's locked and bolted."

"So she's not likely to be able to get out that way, good. That means she's almost certainly trapped down there." That was both good news and bad as far as Nathan was concerned. Good because it meant Dennings was unlikely to get away, and bad because a trapped killer was even more dangerous. "Okay, I want you to stay here and keep that torch focused on the doorway, so I always know where it is. Louisa," he turned to his friend, who had followed him when he hurried down to the ground floor, "I want you and Jenny to go back to reception and keep an eye on the entrance and the stairs in case Dennings is no longer in the cellar and tries to get away."

"If you think I'm letting you go down there alone," Louisa said, eyeing the darkness with concern. "You've got another think coming."

"Don't be stupid, Lou, you're not going down there with me," Nathan told her. "I don't want to have to worry about you on top of where Dennings, Havers and Fulton are."

"Oh right, so I get to worry about you down there, possibly with a murderer." Louisa was far from happy with that idea. "I can just imagine what April and Stephen will have to say if anything happens to you. I'd rather be down there risking bumping into the murderer."

Nathan ground his teeth in frustration. He realised that he should have expected his friend to act as she was, nonetheless he was more than simply put out. It had been enough of a risk to have her along while he searched the rooms, taking her down into the darkened cellar was a risk too far.

Insisting that she stay out of the cellar was not likely to work, though, Louisa would either ignore him and follow on his heels or she would wait for a little bit and then follow him.

"Fine, but on your head be it," he said reluctantly.

The light from the torch in Nathan's hand cut through the darkness like a knife through butter, illuminating boxes, crates and barrels, all of which were stacked neatly on either side of the stairs for easy access. To their left, a short distance from the stack of barrels were those connected to the taps in the bar above, and beyond them was disorder.

Everything that was no longer needed or used by the hotel seemed to have been brought down to the cellar to be stored, with none of the neatness or concern for ease of access that was shown with the drinks and snacks used by the bar. The only element of organisation that was visible amongst the piles of rubbish was an aisle that had been kept clear, presumably because it led to the outside access.

"Can you see any sign of her?" Louisa asked as she stood at Nathan's elbow and peered beyond the torchlight into the darkness, searching for any hint of movement.

"No, nothing so far," Nathan said in a low voice. He didn't want to make any more noise than necessary, though he supposed the precaution was wasted given that the light from his torch must have already revealed his presence. "I can't see any sign of Havers or Fulton either. Of course, if we do see something, chances are it'll turn out to be a mouse or a rat," he told her with perverse humour, for which he was rewarded with a punch to the shoulder.

"Don't say that," Louisa hissed at him. "I've been trying not to think about the possibility of encountering vermin down here." There was a shudder in her voice, one that made it all too clear how much she disliked the possibility, which was at odds with the indifference she normally displayed when it came to the hazards she was likely to encounter while doing her job.

"Better a mouse than a murderer," Nathan remarked. "Hold on, looks like there's something over there."

"What is it?" Louisa asked.

Nathan aimed his light behind the barrels connected to the bar up above but couldn't see enough to identify what he had spotted. "Can't be sure." Stepping off the stairs he cautiously made his way over to the barrels. "Shit!" He swore when he rounded the barrels and saw what it was that had caught his eye.

He dropped to his knees to check on Constable Fulton, who was prostrate on the dirty floor of the cellar. "He's alive," he said after a moment, relief evident in his voice. "Mr Pierson," he called out, getting back to his feet so he could return to the foot of the stairs.

"Yes, inspector?" Pierson called back.

"I've found Constable Fulton, it looks like he's been hit over the head. He's alive, but I can't tell how seriously he's hurt. I need you to call the emergency operator and see if they can get an air ambulance out here. Now the storm's died down some they might be able to make it." He hadn't been happy about not being able to get Helen Moore to hospital yesterday evening, given that she could have been suffering from concussion, bleeding to the brain, or any number of other injuries as a result of her fall down the stairs. They hadn't been able to make a call to the emergency operator then, though, so they couldn't let anyone know that an ambulance was needed. The circumstances were different now, and Nathan was determined that everything possible would be done to get help there.

"I'll get right on it."

"Thanks, and while you're on with the operator, see if you can get the police in town to send some officers out here to help with the search for Dennings, they must have a chopper they can use to airlift some officers in here."

"Okay."

"So, what do we do now?" Louisa asked once Nathan had finished shouting up to Pierson at the top of the stairs.

Nathan took a moment to think about the situation and then said, "You stay here and keep an eye on Fulton, I'll see if I can find Havers or Dennings. I know there's not much you can do for him, but we can't just leave him here unattended."

"I don't think so." Louisa shook her head. "You've got the only torch. If you think I'm going to stay here in the dark with someone who's been bashed over the head, while you search the rest of the cellar, you're nuts. I'm going with you and the torch." She saw Nathan's mouth open and quickly cut him off. "As you said, there's not much I can do for him. Nothing really. So the only thing me staying here in the dark is going to do is make me a target for Dennings, wherever she is."

"Fine," Nathan said resignedly. He could see the logic of what Louisa said, but that didn't mean he liked the thought of leaving Fulton unattended when he had been injured.

For a couple of minutes, he stayed where he was, playing the torch he held around what he could see of the cellar in case Constable Havers was somewhere nearby. He saw no sign of him and concluded that Havers had gone further into the cellar before encountering Dennings, so he left the barrels and began making his way over the piles of furniture and odds and ends in case Havers' body was behind one of them.

A sudden loud bang startled both Nathan and Louisa, making them lose their footing and go down amid a clatter of loose furniture. A second bang spurred them on as they sought to free themselves, and a third came as they pulled themselves, bruised and battered, from the pile that had collapsed on top of them.

Nathan cursed whoever had put the furniture and other unwanted items down there. If they hadn't done so so haphazardly he wouldn't have needed to climb around on the mess in search of the missing constables and Laura Dennings, and he wouldn't now feel as though he had been beaten black and blue by an old wardrobe.

"Where did it come from?" Louisa asked of Nathan as he swung the torch he held left and right, cutting apart the darkness in search of the source of the bangs.

Nathan didn't answer straightaway, he was too busy straining his eyes to see through the darkness. "That way," he said finally when another bang echoed through the darkness. The light from his torch danced up and down, left and right as he hurried through the cluttered cellar towards the source of the noise.

Louisa followed the dancing beam of light, not wanting to get left in the darkness with whatever vermin had made it their home. She hadn't yet seen any proof that there was vermin living in the cellar, but that didn't stop her feeling as though the darkness was made of eyes, watching and waiting for the right moment to pounce. That moment, Louisa was sure, was bound to come when the light was gone.

She was caught by surprise when the light stopped moving and she walked into the back of Nathan, who was so intent on whatever had made him stop that he showed no sign of being aware of the collision.

"What's up?" Louisa asked as her eyes moved along the stationary beam of light towards the object it was aimed at. "Is that...?" Her voice broke off and she couldn't bring herself to finish the question she had started. The pair of black shoes illuminated by the torch made her think the worst, especially when the beam moved up the legs, across the torso and onto the head, which was turned sideways as if to look at one of the piles of abandoned furniture. The side of the face that was uppermost was red from the jawline to just below the eye, revealing that he had been struck with something. "He's not dead, is he?"

Nathan was as concerned by that possibility as Louisa and passing the torch over, so she could illuminate the prostrate constable, he quickly moved forward, lowering himself into a squatting position alongside Havers.

It was hard to tell if the constable's chest was moving, which would have indicated that he was breathing, so Nathan reached out to place two fingers on his throat. He had to move his fingers around a bit, but he eventually found the pulse he was looking for, causing him to sigh in relief.

"He's alive." Nathan told Louisa as he straightened up. "But he needs medical attention urgently. I can't tell how serious his injuries are down here, he could be suffering from just about anything, including internal bleeding, but I think it's clear that he's worse than Fulton. He must have followed Dennings after she attacked Fulton and then got attacked as well."

"So where's Dennings now?" Louisa asked. Her eyes darted rapidly around the dark cellar as though she expected Dennings to suddenly jump out at them, brandishing whatever it was she had hit the two constables with.

"The hatch that leads outside," Nathan said as the thought occurred to him like the proverbial thunderbolt. "That must be what the banging was. It must have been Dennings trying to force it open."

"She can't have succeeded, though, can she?" Louisa asked. "Pierson said it's locked and bolted; if she had somehow managed to get it open, we'd have seen a patch of daylight somewhere around here, so she's got to still be down here. You can't keep looking for her on your own. Just look at what she did to Fulton and Havers, and to that cook

— she's clearly very dangerous. You're going to get yourself hurt," she said in concern.

As if her words were a signal, the banging started up again, louder and with greater intensity.

It was the sound of desperation and both Nathan and Louisa turned to where the noise was coming from. They could see nothing initially, not even with the help of the torch, but that soon changed. A sudden burst of dim daylight followed the last bang, a sure sign that Laura Dennings had succeeded in busting open the hatch. A silhouette against the daylight, one which disappeared as quickly as it appeared, revealed that Dennings had indeed succeeded in making her escape from the previously secure hotel.

Nathan reacted instinctively the moment he saw the silhouette. "Get Pierson to call search and rescue," he told Louisa over his shoulder as he scrambled over the furniture towards the aisle that led to the delivery hatch. "If she's gone outside we might need them."

"What're you doing?" Louisa called after Nathan. "Nathan. Nate! Come back. Don't be stupid, you can't go chasing after her on your own." Her words fell on deaf ears and she was forced to watch in the light from the torch she held as Nathan raced away. He disappeared briefly behind a stack of furniture before reappearing as an outline on his way through the delivery hatch, visible as a darker area against the backdrop of the not quite black sky and the pouring rain.

Nathan's departure left Louisa torn as to what she should do. She wanted to chase after Nathan but had to get Pierson to call for the search and rescue people, and she needed to keep an eye on Constables Havers and Fulton.

Ultimately, indecision kept her frozen in place until she heard David Pierson calling for Nathan. His voice made her mind up and she left the badly injured Havers, so she could return to the hotel proper.

31

After the slightly claustrophobic atmosphere of the dark cellar Nathan felt good being outside, even if he was soaked in seconds and buffeted by the wind.

He only allowed himself as long as it took him to look around and spot the fleeing figure to appreciate being outside again, though. The moment he saw Dennings and knew in which direction she was heading, he set off after in pursuit.

As always when he was forced to take part in a foot chase, he found himself wishing that he was in better shape. It wasn't that he was out of shape, though he acknowledged that his fitness had taken a dip over the past year, it was just that he knew if he were to spend even a bit of time on a regular exercise regime he could be so much fitter.

The hatch through which the deliveries for the bar were made opened onto the hotel's rear car park, and on the far side of it were the woods that bordered the moor. It was into those woods that Laura Dennings had run, presumably because they offered the closest avenue of escape.

Nathan entered the woods in the same spot as Laura Dennings and scanned the gaps between the trees for some sign of the fleeing murderess. The instant he caught a glimpse of her he set off in pursuit, hoping that it wouldn't take him long to catch her. The rain, which continued to lash down, though not as fiercely as it had yesterday, cut visibility drastically, making it hard to keep his target in sight.

Not only did the rain leave him worried that Dennings would get away from him, it raised the possibility that he would fall or injure himself, either because he didn't see a hazard in time to avoid it or because the damp caused his muscles to cramp up. He was less concerned that something similar might happen to Dennings, since if it did he would have an easier time catching her.

As he ran, dodging between trees and ducking under low branches, Nathan reflected on how badly he had underestimated the killer he was pursuing. He had dismissed Elizabeth Creek as too mousy, too bookish to be a murderer; he hadn't even considered the possibility that how she acted might be a pose, a cover.

It wasn't like him to underestimate someone so badly, and he could only conclude that it was because he was still on holiday when he formed his impression of her, though that was no excuse.

Fifteen minutes after the chase began, during which time Nathan was sure he received more minor injuries than he had in the last couple of years, thanks to the branches, bushes and other foliage that caught at his clothes and skin, he didn't seem any closer to Dennings than at the start of the chase.

He hadn't been able to cut the distance because it was impossible for him to try and anticipate her. She was slowly but surely moving further into the woods, heading towards the moor, but seemed to have no real idea of where she was going.

The chase got a little easier for Nathan when they reached the path he had followed days before while exploring the countryside around the village. The distance between them was about fifty feet, Nathan saw as Dennings disappeared around the bend where he had encountered Tracey Pierson the night she was murdered, less than he had thought when he entered the woods. He worried that she was going to disappear into the woods again the moment she was out of sight, but that soon proved not to be a problem.

Nathan had no idea whether Dennings was unaware that he was behind her, was confident in her ability to outrun him, or if she simply thought that she was better off sticking to the path. Whatever it was, she made no attempt to evade him, she simply followed the path that ran parallel to the river, which Nathan knew would lead them past the small waterfall and up onto the moor.

He knew that because of his explorations. He also knew that once they reached the moor, Dennings' chances of getting away would diminish dramatically. Even with the rain reducing visibility he would be able to see her from farther away.

Barring an accident, or her leaving the path to re-enter the woods, Nathan felt confident that it was only a matter of time before he caught Dennings.

No sooner had he thought that than he caught his foot on something and went down with a loud exclamation. He rolled once and then slid along the path, the surface of which had been turned to mud by two days of persistent rain, for about half a dozen feet.

He groaned when he came to a stop and attempted to push himself up. His hands sank into the gloop that covered the path and it took an effort to pull them free.

He caught a glimpse of Dennings as he struggled against the mud. She appeared to have stopped and to be looking back at him, but when he looked up again she was gone, which made him wonder if he had just imagined it.

His heart leapt into his mouth when a hand grabbed hold of him and hauled him, unceremoniously, to his feet. It beat there in a rapid tempo that made him think he was about to have a heart attack.

When he saw that it was Louisa who had helped him up he felt foolish.

"Where would you be without me?" Louisa asked. She looked him up and down and shook her head at the state of him; he was covered in mud from head to toe, to such an extent that she could no longer tell what clothes he was wearing, let alone the colour of them. If he was injured, and she was sure he must be, his injuries weren't visible.

"Still stuck in the mud, for a guess," Nathan said as he made a half-hearted, and utterly futile, attempt to brush off some of the mud he was caked in.

"Probably," Louisa agreed. "This stuff is like glue." As if to emphasise her words she lifted a foot, no easy task since the mud clung to her shoe, threatening to pull it from her foot and keep it prisoner. "Are you alright? Did you do any damage when you fell?"

Nathan nodded. "Don't ask me where, though," he said with a prolonged wince as he probed gingerly at his body to try and localise the injuries he could feel. He had no success, however; it felt as though the pain was coming from just about every part of his anatomy. "I think it's going to take about ten showers just to find my skin, let alone whatever injuries I've got."

"You'd better come back with me then," Louisa told him. "Pierson's got the air ambulance on its way from Chilton, and the local search and rescue, and some officers from the police station. Apparently, they're all coming in choppers, so they should be here soon. We should be able to get you cleaned up enough for the paramedics to figure out what injuries you've got and how bad they are by the time they get here."

Nathan was torn. His body was strongly in favour of doing what Louisa was suggesting, he hurt, his whole body ached, he was soaking wet and covered in mud, and he was as tired as if he had run several times as far as he had. On the flip side there was his determination not to give up on catching Dennings while he was still mobile enough to give chase.

His brain told him that continuing the chase was futile, Dennings was out of sight, who knew how far ahead, and getting further away with every passing moment. It was even possible, likely, if she had the slightest bit of smarts about her, that she had left the path and was heading in who knew what direction through the woods.

"Did you hear that?" Nathan's head whipped around as he asked the question of Louisa. It had been barely audible, covered almost totally by the wind as it whipped through the trees, raising a racket from the branches and the leaves, yet Nathan was sure he had heard a cry for help.

Louisa cocked her head to one side and listened for a few moments. "All I can hear is the wind and the trees. Come on, let's get out of here. The search and rescue guys can look for Dennings with the local police, they're better suited to it, especially now she's out here in the wilds," she said with a look around at their surroundings. She knew the countryside they were in wasn't all that wild, certainly not compared to the countryside in other places around the world, but it was wild enough for an urbanite like herself.

"There it is again," Nathan said as the high, thin, and desperate sound reached his ears for a second time. It was pitched at just the right level to carry under or through the wind, though it was only just possible to make out that it was human in origin. The words that made up the sound, if it was made of words, were impossible to make out, though.

"I can't hear a..." Louisa stopped speaking when she realised that Nathan wasn't listening to her, he was lumbering along the path as quickly as his rain-soaked and mud-encrusted clothes would allow, which was barely half his usual top speed. "Dammit, Nate, why d'you always have to be such a bloody idiot?" she asked of the wind and the rain as she set off after her friend.

She knew she should be used to the way her friend thought, and how he was likely to react to any situation that arose, but she was still surprised that he had gone running off into the storm after a noise only he had heard.

Louisa caught up to Nathan after only thirty yards, her movements less impeded than his since she was only struggling with waterlogged clothes, not clothes heavily laden with mud.

She was about to take Nathan by the arm and haul him to a halt out of fear that he was making his injuries worse when she saw movement up ahead. The rain made it difficult for her to be sure what she was seeing, but since the blobs of colour that were visible didn't match anything that lived or grew in the area she guessed that it was a person, and that almost certainly made it Dennings.

"Over there." She pointed as she shouted, to make sure Nathan didn't miss what she had seen.

Nathan slowed so he could peer through the wind and the rain in the direction Louisa was pointing. He had to blink several times to clear his vision for they had reached an area where the trees thinned as the path turned to run alongside a stream, then crossed it to follow the river for a while before curving away and up the promontory over which the river cascaded.

With nothing to shelter them from the elements, the wind whipped the rain painfully into their faces, almost blinding them, but Nathan eventually managed to clear his vision enough to see what it was that Louisa was trying to show him.

"Come on," he said urgently, starting off again, moving quicker than before. "She's in trouble."

Louisa had gathered that much from the small amount she could see, though if she was honest she couldn't see how that was a reason for them to move quickly. Dennings had killed at least two people and caused a lot of trouble for people who were already enduring a bad holiday because of the weather; getting herself in trouble while trying to escape was entirely her own fault, and no reason for the two of them to risk themselves.

Tempted as she was, she said nothing of what she thought to Nathan. He wouldn't think too highly of her for it and besides, it was clear that he had already made up his mind by the fact that he had established a lead of a dozen or so yards on her.

Reluctantly, and unhappily, Louisa followed her friend. She sincerely hoped it wasn't a decision she was going to regret.

She suspected she was going to have regrets when she saw Nathan enter the stream, which had grown significantly thanks to the persistent rain of the past couple of days. It only came up to just below his knees, but it was faster and more powerful than he expected and his arms windmilled wildly as his legs were nearly swept out from under him. Seeing that, Louisa balked at the thought of following him.

It required no imagination for her to realise what would happen if she lost her footing. She would be swept into the river, which was only a short distance away, and once in the river her chances of saving herself were likely to be too long for even the most risk-taking of gamblers to put money on it, especially with it running as high and as fast as it was.

When Nathan kept going after recovering his balance, without even looking over his shoulder, Louisa took the plunge and followed him. She stepped into the stream, bracing herself against the rushing water; it beat and swirled against her legs insistently, desperately trying to upend her. She resisted it with every step as she edged towards the other side and then uttered a silent prayer of thanks when she reached it without incident.

She was relieved that the stream, swollen as it was, was only four feet wide. If it had been any wider she wasn't sure she would have stayed on her feet. The shifting stones under her feet were as much of a danger as the current.

Louisa's legs trembled uncontrollably as she regained the path and resumed her pursuit of Nathan. She felt certain that they were going to give out on her at any moment, yet she kept going, determined not to leave her friend in case he got stuck again, or had an accident. The storm might be past its worst, but if anything happened to Nathan and he was on his own there was every chance that he would die of exposure before help could find him.

Fortunately, she only had to follow Nathan for about a quarter of a mile after the path reached the moor.

A portion of the path where it followed the edge of the cliff near the waterfall had collapsed, undoubtedly worn away by the wind and the rain, and Nathan quickly dropped to his knees, so he could crawl to the edge.

"Are you alright?" he called down to Elizabeth Creek/ Laura Dennings, who was desperately clinging to the face of the cliff. From his position, Nathan couldn't tell if she was more likely to hit the ground at the base of the cliff or the pool that the waterfall spilled into after cascading the forty feet from the moor. He suspected it wouldn't make much difference where she landed; her chances of surviving, given the conditions, were probably about the same — not good. "Hold on, help's on the way."

Nathan wriggled back from the edge and looked around for Louisa. "Have you got your phone?" he asked when he saw her.

Louisa nodded. "What do you want me to do?" She was careful not to get too close to where the path had collapsed, she had no desire to put herself at risk of being caught in a further slip and finding herself alongside the murder suspect.

"Call Pierson and tell him the situation and that we're at the waterfall, he can relay our location to the search and rescue team," Nathan told her. He turned his attention back to Laura Dennings then, whom he estimated was about ten feet down from his position, and thirty feet up from the ground, far enough for her life to be in danger. "The search and rescue people are on their way, they should be here soon," he called down.

"They'd better hurry," Laura Dennings called back up, a note of panic in her voice. "I'm not sure how much longer I can hold on."

32

Nathan's prediction of soon proved to be an overestimation. It was almost half an hour before the helicopter bearing the search and rescue team appeared in the sky overhead. During that time Laura Dennings clung desperately to the protruding piece of rock that was all that kept her from plummeting to either injury or death. It became increasingly hard to manage as the rain continued to pour down for the face of the cliff, already slick from two days of persistent precipitation, became wetter and more precarious.

While Louisa remained a safe distance from the edge, fearful that it would give way again, Nathan stayed where he was, so he could offer reassurance to Dennings, all he could do from his position. He also wanted to keep an eye on her in case she should make a crazy and potentially suicidal attempt to escape.

Laura Dennings proved to have better sense than to do anything other than cling on for dear life, for which he was glad. Had she tried to get away he would have felt obliged to stop her, or at least to attempt to do so, and he was sure that one or both of them would get injured, almost certainly seriously, if not killed in the process.

The relief Nathan felt at first hearing and then seeing the helicopter that brought help was short-lived. The downdraft as it flew over the top of him at a height of twenty-five feet pressed him into the muddy ground and made him feel as though he was going to become a part of the path. It also made it incredibly difficult to breathe, and momentarily robbed him of both vision and hearing.

When his senses returned he saw that Dennings had also been affected by the downdraft. Her grip, which she had already been dangerously close to losing, was now all but gone; she was clutching onto the rock with one hand, while she scrabbled frantically against the face of the cliff with the other, seeking something, anything, she could grab hold of to avoid plummeting to her death.

"Help!"

Nathan could not recall an occasion when he had felt as useless as he did then. He could see Laura Dennings desperately holding on for dear life, but there was nothing he could do to help her. No matter how precarious his position, he couldn't reach her, and he had nothing he could extend to overcome the gap between them. All he could do was wait for the search and rescue team to save Dennings.

Half a minute after its first pass the helicopter returned. The downdraft from the rapidly spinning rotor blades again forced Nathan into the ground, pressed his soaked clothing tight to his body, and took his breath away. It required every ounce of strength he could muster to get himself into a kneeling position, he didn't even try to get to his feet, and once he managed it he looked up at the helicopter.

The turbulence the helicopter created buffeted him and made him blink rapidly. He felt as though his eyeballs were being pushed back into his skull, but he was able to make out the figure at the open side door of the helicopter.

Nathan raised a hand to try and shield himself, while with the other he pointed over the edge of the path to indicate where the person in need of rescue was. A second later the helicopter shifted position, so it was hovering just beyond the edge of the small cliff. He had no idea if he had been seen, or if the man at the door had seen Laura Dennings for himself, but it didn't matter, all that did was that she had been spotted.

Certain that the rescue was now underway, Nathan cautiously crawled backwards to safety. He didn't stop until he bumped into Louisa's legs, at which point he slowly, and with difficulty because of the strength of the mud's suction and the weight of his sodden clothes, got to his feet.

"I sometimes wonder if you've got the sense God gave a two-year-old," Louisa said almost conversationally once Nathan joined her. "Did you think, even for a moment, that you were risking your life for someone who would almost certainly have tried to knock you off if your positions had been reversed? What would you have done if the path had collapsed under you?"

Nathan shrugged as he tore his attention away from the helicopter, which was lowering someone on a winch. "Fallen, I imagine, and most likely been seriously hurt or killed," he said in a tone which stopped just short of being blasé. "What was I supposed to do?" he asked. "Leave her for the elements? Maybe give her a chance to get away, if she was stupid enough to try it? I couldn't do either of those things."

Louisa opened her mouth to say something in response to that but a look at her friend made her shut it again with a snap. It would be a waste of time, she realised, to try and make Nathan admit that he had risked his life stupidly or unnecessarily; she knew that had there been a realistic chance of him succeeding, Nathan would have tried to rescue Laura Dennings, even if it risked his own life.

Since there was nothing she could say just then, on that subject or any other, Louisa remained silent, watching, as Nathan did, while the search and rescue team completed the rescue of Laura Dennings.

FIVE MINUTES AFTER the search and rescue team member was lowered on the winch, he was raised, with Laura Dennings clinging to him. She continued to do so as the cable was wound in, so she and her rescuer could be assisted to safety.

Once they were both on board the helicopter it crabbed sideways until it was over safe ground, a distance from the now treacherous path.

As Nathan watched the helicopter land, he wondered if it was a good idea for it to do so. It seemed unlikely, but he worried that it would get stuck in the mud and not be able to take off again. If that happened they would likely be there until the rain stopped and the mud dried out, or until someone could get to them with a spade.

He was distracted from that concern when a figure jumped out from the helicopter and hurried over to him, ducking low under the rotors.

"Charlie Hutch, Devonshire search and rescue," the figure introduced himself briskly. "Which one of you is Inspector Stone?"

Nathan assumed that the guy hadn't been told that Inspector Stone was male, otherwise there wouldn't have been any confusion. "That's me," he said, holding out a hand to the man. "Thanks for getting here so quickly, I'm not sure how much longer she could have held on for."

"No problem, that's what we're here for," Hutch said. "It helps when we know exactly where we've got to go. I was told the lady who needed rescuing is a suspect of some kind, is that right?"

Nathan nodded. He could tell that Hutch was curious to know what sort of crime Dennings was suspected of, but he decided that it would be best not to tell the man that he had just rescued a suspected murderer.

"Okay, well, you'd better come with us, sir, you too, miss," Hutch said to Louisa. "We've got to take the lady to hospital, she doesn't appear to be injured but she is suffering from shock, and if she's a suspect she needs a police escort. You look as though you could do with being checked out as well."

Nathan nodded, even if he hadn't needed to go with them to keep an eye on Dennings, in case she tried to escape, he would have wanted to hitch a lift, so he could get cleaned up and have his numerous, hopefully minor, injuries checked out as soon as possible.

Stiff-legged, as though he was in casts from hip to ankle, he followed Hutch to the helicopter, with Louisa at his side. He had to be helped into the helicopter but soon enough he was strapped in safely opposite Laura Dennings, who was soaked, shivering, and clearly in shock from her traumatic experience.

From what he could see, Dennings was in no fit state to even think about escaping, let alone physically capable of attempting it. Despite that, Nathan was glad that she was hemmed in on either side by two members of the search and rescue team.

No sooner was the door closed than Nathan felt the power of the engine as it was started up and the rotors began turning. The entire helicopter seemed to shake, making his teeth rattle, and he clenched them tight to keep them still as he distracted himself by looking out the window. "What a holiday," he sighed.

"What was that, sir?" Hutch asked loudly.

Nathan flushed, embarrassed that he had been overheard. "Nothing," he said quickly. "I was just speaking to myself."

"Okay." Hutch glanced at Dennings briefly and then looked back to Nathan. "Shouldn't she be in cuffs?" He tried to ask the question discreetly, but that was difficult when he had to almost shout to be heard over the engine.

"Yes, but I don't have any." Nathan regretted not taking the cuffs from the belt of Constable Havers' uniform, but under the circumstances he didn't feel as though he could blame himself for not doing so. "It's been a crazy morning," he said by way of explanation. *And a crazy few days*, he added silently. "Can your pilot radio ahead and have uniformed officers meet us at the hospital?"

Hutch nodded. "It'll take us a while to get there, so they should make it to the hospital ahead of us."

"Good. I don't want her to have a chance to get away." Nathan remembered the police backup he had requested, which he assumed had gone to the hotel, if they had been sent. He would have liked to have some of them with him, but he supposed, given the situation at the hotel, they would be able to find something to do.

As the helicopter ascended and turned to head to town he settled back to enjoy the ride, which wasn't easy since they were being buffeted by the wind and the rain. His relaxed posture didn't mean he wasn't keeping an eye on Laura Dennings; anyone who would run out into a storm, even if it was past its worst, to escape the police was likely to take any opportunities that came along to get away and he wasn't about to let that happen. It would be embarrassing to have her escape after what it had taken to identify and catch her.

33

"Nate, it's Stephen, for you." Louisa had to speak twice and then nudge Nathan to get his attention.

"Huh, what?" Nathan blinked and looked around to see what it was that had disturbed him. After being examined by both a nurse and a doctor he had been given a strong enough dose of painkillers to be left feeling numb and detached from things. Thankfully, his injuries were relatively minor, mostly just bumps and bruises, but there were plenty of them thanks to the furniture that had crashed down on him in the cellar of The Moor's Edge, and the skidding fall he had taken in the woods.

"Phone for you, it's Stephen," Louisa said, holding out her mobile.

"Why is he calling me on your phone?" Nathan asked.

"No idea, why don't you ask him."

"Good idea." Nathan took the phone from his friend. "Hi, Stephen. How come you're calling me on Lou's phone?"

"Because yours is going straight to the answerphone," Stephen told him. "Did you forget to charge it or something?"

"No." Taking his phone from his pocket, Nathan saw that it was off. He tried to turn it on but got no response, the screen didn't even try to light up. "I think it might be broken." That wouldn't surprise him given it had had to put up with all the rain and mud that morning; most phones would give up the ghost after that. "What's up?"

"I've got that information you were after, some of it anyway. Can you talk?"

Nathan looked around. He was sitting outside the private room where Laura Dennings had been placed; nurses, doctors, and porters walked past every so often but paid no attention to him, while in the room, two uniformed officers kept watch over the handcuffed suspect.

"Sure, what have you found?" He hoped his friend had found something useful. He might have a suspect in custody, but he didn't yet have enough evidence to secure a conviction, and that was a lack that troubled him. He was going to be glad when the forensics people were able to get to the village and begin their work; thankfully, the scene of Jean Martin's murder had been preserved, so there should be no problem resulting from the delay.

If there was evidence to connect Elizabeth Creek/ Laura Dennings to the murder of the man he believed to be her husband, he was confident it would be found.

"Jean Martin, your murdered chef, is actually John Martin, a cook from Portsmouth," Stephen said. "I've made a few calls and spoken to a few people who knew him, and they told me he started calling himself Jean after getting divorced. He also began giving out the story that he was French and began fudging his qualifications and experience as a cook. It seems that he is a very good cook, but his resumé is exaggerated, to say the least.

"The resumé padding was obviously to help him get work, but the name change was apparently so it would be harder for his ex-wife to find him. It wasn't done officially, though."

That was useful information, but didn't help the investigation, especially since he had already discovered that Jean Martin was actually John Martin from the divorce papers found in his room, so Nathan asked, "What about the ex-wife? Have you been able to find out anything about her?"

"Some. Her married name was Laura Martin, maiden name, Laura Dennings, a part-time actress. The Portsmouth police have her in their system, they've been called out three times because of reports of domestic abuse — the calls were made by her neighbours. Two incidents involved her husband, John Martin, and the third involved a former fiancé. On all three occasions it was believed that Laura Dennings was the abuser, but no charges were ever filed because of a lack of support from either man." That didn't surprise Stephen, and he was sure it wouldn't surprise Nathan either; men were even more reluctant to file charges against a domestic abuser than women because of the stigma attached to being the victim of such a crime. "John Martin did start the process of getting a restraining order against his wife following the divorce but dropped it for some reason."

"Was she fingerprinted, or DNA sampled at any point?" Nathan asked hopefully.

"Both."

"That's good, I'll be able to confirm her identity then."

"I can save you some time," Stephen said. "I've sent a copy of her mugshot to your email."

"Thanks. Were you able to find out anything else?"

"HELLO, MS DENNINGS, I'm Detective Inspector Stone, in case you weren't aware," Nathan greeted the woman in the bed. "It is Ms Dennings, isn't it? Ms Laura Dennings. This is your bank card." He held up the bank card Louisa and Jennifer Pierson had found, which Louisa had had in her pocket throughout the pursuit of the fleeing murder suspect. "We found it in the room you booked under the name Elizabeth Creek."

The woman, who no longer appeared so mousy or librarian-looking as she had when he first saw her in the hotel dining room, stared at him without saying anything. There was malevolence in her look that made

Nathan think she must be a better than average actor to have concealed it so well during her stay at The Moor's Edge.

"There's no point denying who you are," Nathan continued. "Not only do we have your bank card, we have your picture from your police file," he held up Louisa's phone to show the photo Stephen had emailed, "and in a short while we'll be able to confirm your identity through fingerprints and DNA."

Consternation flickered across her face. "Fine, yes, I'm Laura Dennings," she said.

"Thank you. Now, I'm sure you realise that you're in a lot of trouble, and the best thing you can do is cooperate if you want to minimise that trouble, so, let's talk about what happened at The Moor's Edge hotel.

"You were stalking your ex-husband, John Martin, weren't you, and you took pictures of him with his lover, Tracey Pierson, pictures that you sent to David Pierson in the hopes of ending the affair, after sending threatening messages to Tracey Pierson to try and get her to stop it herself."

"Yes," Laura Dennings admitted with a quick, abrupt nod of her head. "She ignored me to begin with, and then, when I threatened to tell her husband about the affair, she told me I was a sad, pathetic woman who should accept my marriage was over and not interfere with other people's lives. Then she told me she had got her hands on the pictures I sent, and her husband remained unaware of the affair, that I was wasting my time and acting like a pathetic, jealous bitch." She flushed angrily at the memory.

"Is that when you decided to kill her?" Nathan asked.

"No," Laura said sharply. "I didn't plan on killing her. It never even occurred to me. I just wanted David back."

"So why did you book into the hotel under a false name, if you weren't planning on killing Tracey Pierson?"

"I had to use a false name. I knew if I didn't that Pierson bitch would keep me away, she'd cancel my booking or do something else to stop me. All I wanted was to get David back. I thought if I went to the hotel I could convince him to come back with me."

"What happened?"

"He wasn't interested. That Pierson bitch had him bewitched. She enticed him with nude pictures and kept him in her snare with sex. I realised if I was going to get him back I was going to have to split them up. I tried to talk to her husband, to tell him what his wife was up to, but he never seemed to be around, and when he was he was too busy to talk to me."

"That must have been frustrating," Nathan said. "Is that what finally led you to kill Tracey Pierson?"

"No. I told you, I didn't plan on killing her. I saw her go out into the woods that night and followed her. I figured she was going to meet John. I already had the pictures I tried to send David Pierson, but they weren't very good; I thought I might be able to get some better pictures or maybe some video, then I could force David Pierson to listen to me and see what his wife is up to. I hoped that that'd be the end of the affair and I'd get John back."

"But all they did is talk, right."

"Uh huh. They didn't even say much that was likely to convince Pierson his wife was having an affair, you came along before they could. I had to wait until John and you had gone, since I didn't want to be seen, then I headed back to the hotel. Somehow Pierson got back to the hotel before me, don't ask me how. She was the one who let me in, and somehow she knew who I was." Laura fell silent for a few moments before continuing. "I don't really know what happened after that, we ended up arguing in the hotel kitchen and then Pierson was on the floor and I was standing over her with the tenderiser in my hand.

"I expected someone to come in and catch me, I was sure someone must have heard us arguing, but no-one came. When I realised I wasn't going to get caught I spent some time trying to figure out what to do; I decided to take Pierson's body out to the woods. I figured it would be a while before she was found, if she was found, and if I was lucky I'd be long gone before she was."

"Why didn't you just leave the next morning?" Nathan asked curiously. "You were booked in under a false name, chances are, if you'd left straightaway you'd have got away with it."

"I was sure I could get John back, especially with Pierson gone."

It didn't surprise Nathan that that was why Dennings had stuck around, it was clear that she was obsessed with her ex-husband and he featured heavily in her thinking, regardless of the situation.

"How did you get Tracey Pierson's body out to the woods?" he asked. "Did you have help?"

"No."

Nathan looked at her dubiously. "Are you sure? Tracey Pierson wasn't a big person, but she was bigger than you, and her body was found a couple of miles from the hotel. Do you expect me to believe that you managed to carry her body to where it was found all by yourself?"

Laura nodded. "I'm stronger than I look. It took an effort, and I was bloody knackered afterwards, but I managed it on my own."

For the time being, Nathan accepted what she said since he had other questions he wanted to ask. "Okay, so you killed Tracey Pierson during an argument and you took her body out to the woods to keep her from being found easily, which didn't work out too well for you, and you stuck around afterwards because you hoped to convince your ex-husband to go home with you. Have I got that all clear so far?"

"Yes."

"INSPECTOR STONE?"

The query made Nathan look up in time to see two people stop in front of him, one of whom wore the uniform of a police superintendent. He immediately got to his feet. He would have leapt were he not too tired and sore for such exertions; he took comfort from the fact that he could at least move with relative ease now that he was dressed in clean, dry clothes.

"Yes, sir."

"Superintendent Rainer, Devonshire Constabulary," the immaculately uniformed officer identified himself. "This is Detective Inspector Kellogg." He made a brief gesture to the woman at his side. "I'm given to understand you have caught the person responsible for the murder you were asked to investigate in Donningford."

"Yes, sir. A woman by the name of Laura Dennings. I don't have proof positive yet, but she has confessed to me that she killed Tracey Pierson and her ex-husband, John Martin."

"That's good." Rainer nodded in satisfaction. "So, all that's left is filling in a few blanks and the forensics work. If you don't mind, now that Donningford is accessible again, albeit only by helicopter, I'd like Inspector Kellogg to take over and finish things off."

"Of course, sir. I have no objections," Nathan said, knowing that it would be pointless for him to say anything even if he did have objections. He had been drafted to help during an emergency, and while that emergency wasn't over, it was diminished enough for him to no longer be needed.

"Good, then I'll leave you to fill Kellogg in on all the details and make sure she's one hundred percent up to date on everything that's happened and everything that needs to be done. Once that's done you can get back to your holiday. Kellogg, I'll expect a report later today on the situation." With that Superintendent Rainer turned and strode briskly away down the passage.

"I'm sorry about this," Kellogg said once her superior had disappeared around the corner and couldn't hear her. "You've done all the hard work, and now you're being yanked off the case and I'm going to get the credit for solving it. It's not my idea," she hastened to reassure Nathan. "It's just that now we can get to the village, the superintendent thinks the investigation should be handled by a local detective. He doesn't like the idea that someone might suggest his officers can't handle a murder investigation."

"It's okay. I'm happy for you to take over, so I can get back to my holiday." *Not that it's likely to be much of a holiday*, he thought. Given the storm and the murders, he doubted there was going to be much entertainment to be had in the village, and he couldn't help wondering if he wouldn't be better off going back to Branton and returning to work.

"Thank you. If you don't mind, I have a few things I need to clear up before I'm ready to take over this case. Rainer kind of rushed me over here the moment he heard what was going on and didn't give me any time to organise myself." When Nathan nodded she went on. "I'll be back as soon as I can, then we can head to the village. Apparently, the chopper is available to me whenever I need it to get to and from the village while the investigation is ongoing — unless there's an emergency, of course."

"Okay. One thing before you go," Nathan said quickly before Kellogg could leave. "How are Constables Havers and Fulton?"

Kellogg looked blankly. "I'm afraid I have no idea. I don't even know who they are. Something else I'll have to be brought up to date on. Once I have some information, I'll let you know."

"Thank you."

"She didn't even ask if there's anyone watching your suspect," Louisa remarked when Kellogg had gone. "Neither of them did. That's a bit of an oversight, isn't it."

"A bit, yes," Nathan agreed. "Fortunately, there is, so it doesn't matter. What are you going to do now that all the excitement's over? Are you going to stick around or go back to Branton?"

"I'm sticking around," Louisa said without hesitation. "I came down to write a story about ocelots and that story isn't finished. I want to know if they've survived the storm, and whatever else Floyd Mantle can tell me about them. Plus, I now have a double murder to write about, and a bunch of human-interest stories from the people who have been affected by this storm. I can get enough material over the next week to keep my site full for a month, if not longer. What about you, are you going to stick around, or are you going back to Branton? It's pretty clear you'd rather be at work than on holiday."

"I was starting to enjoy myself before the storm and the murders," Nathan said defensively. "Besides, even if I wanted to, I can't go back to Branton yet, it's going to take me a while to get Kellogg up to date on everything that's happened. I'm going to be around for at least another day. We'll see how I feel, and what the situation is, after that."

"At least you managed to catch the killer before the case was taken off you."

"Yeah, that's something, I guess. Come on, let's see about some coffee, since it seems as though we're going to be here for a while, waiting for Kellogg to come back so we can return to Donningford." Pushing himself up he walked slowly down the corridor to go in search of the coffee shop he had seen mentioned on a sign when he was following Laura Dennings and her uniformed escort to the private room she had been assigned.

Don't miss out!

Did you love *A Stone's Throw*? Then you should read *Written In Blood* by Alex R Carver!

A peaceful village torn apart by murder, mistrust, and a desire for revenge.

When Oakhurst's daughters begin to turn up, brutally murdered and with accusatory words carved into their skin, the residents of the small, close-knit community are unwilling to believe that one of their own might be a killer.

Suspicion falls on the village's newest resident, Zack Wild, attractive, charming, author of violent crime novels, and possessor of a dark history; he seems like the perfect suspect.

As the investigation continues, the evidence against Wild mounts, but is prejudice against the newcomer affecting the judgment of Sergeant Mitchell, Constable Turner thinks so, and is prepared to do whatever she must to find the killer, whoever it might be.

Who will be proved right, the sergeant or the constable? And will they catch the killer before he can strike again?

Read more at https://alexrcarver.wordpress.com/.

Also by Alex R Carver

Cas Dragunov
An Unwanted Inheritance

Inspector Stone Mysteries
Where There's a Will
An Eye For An Eye
A Perfect Pose
Into The Fire
A Stone's Throw

The Oakhurst Murders
Written In Blood
Poetic Justice

Standalone
Exposed
Inspector Stone Mysteries Volume 1 (Books 1-3)
The Oakhurst Murders Duology

Watch for more at https://alexrcarver.wordpress.com/.

About the Author

After working in the clerical, warehouse and retail industries over the years, without gaining much satisfaction, Alex quit to follow his dream and become a full-time writer. Where There's A Will is the first book in the Inspector Stone Mysteries series, with more books in the series to come, as well as titles in other genres in the pipeline. His dream is to one day earn enough to travel, with a return to Egypt to visit the parts he missed before, and Macchu Picchu, top of his wishlist of destinations. When not writing, he is either playing a game or being distracted by Molly the Yorkie, who is greedy for both attention and whatever food is to be found.

You can find out more about Alex R Carver at the following links

https://twitter.com/arcarver87

https://alexrcarver.wordpress.com/

https://medium.com/@arcarver87

https://www.facebook.com/Alex-R-Carver-1794038897591918/

Read more at https://alexrcarver.wordpress.com/.

Lightning Source UK Ltd.
Milton Keynes UK
UKHW010649230122
397577UK00001B/145

9 781386 089094